the Wish List 2

Keep Calm and Sparkle On!

the Wish List

1. The Worst Fairy Godmother Ever!

2. Keep Calm and Sparkle On!

the Wish List 2

Keep Calm and Sparkle On!

By Sarah Aronson

Scholastic Press
New York

Library of Congress Cataloging-in-Publication Data available

ISBN 978-0-545-94159-4

10 9 8 7 6 5 4 3 2 1   18 19 20 21 22

Printed in the U.S.A.   23

First edition, January 2018

Book design by Maeve Norton

For the real Elizabeth Marie

Chapter One

Happily Ever After, Happily Ever After Not

Dear Trainee, Welcome to Level Two! This is a friendly reminder to bring your wand and any remaining sparkles with you on Day One. Also, be sure to review the rule book, front to back. As always, we appreciate your cooperation! —The Bests

Isabelle sat on her bed and plucked the petals off the last drooping flower. As each one fluttered to the floor, she whispered, "She's happily ever after. She's happily ever after not."

Although she should have been busy getting ready for training (in other words, studying), Isabelle was stuck in a rut. Ever since the night of the Extravaganza—the big party at the end of every fairy godmother season—she hadn't done anything, not even the things she enjoyed most. Things like chasing puffy clouds, running so fast it felt like flying, or snacking on yummy treats like chocolate puffs or strawberry swizzles. Isabelle even avoided the place she loved most: the cozy spot between the girlgoyles, the two stone gargoyles that looked like girls.

It wasn't because she was mad at the girlgoyles.

Or because she felt particularly guilty for trying to break Rule Three C—the rule that said that *after the Extravaganza, all practice princesses will forget their fairy godmothers, no exceptions.*

Rather, it was because her foolproof plan was turning out not to be so foolproof after all.

Back in Level One, Isabelle had barely managed to make Nora happily ever after by, of all things, becoming her friend. This may not seem very magical, but Nora was a regular girl (and not a princess) and Isabelle wasn't all that studious. This still should have been the perfect end of the story, but then Isabelle learned about Rule Three C and had to do something fast. So she snuck out of the Extravaganza back down to Nora's house and left her an entire jar of magic-making sparkles (the ones Isabelle stole from Grandmomma) just in case Nora ever needed her.

Even Isabelle knew that leaving sparkles for a regular girl was against the rules. So to make sure there were no misunderstandings or slipups, Isabelle left them in Nora's memory box. She wrote a detailed note complete with instructions on how to use them. When she was done, she felt a bit smug. She figured she and Nora would be back together in no more than a couple of hours, maybe one day, tops.

But now vacation was almost over, and there'd been

nothing. No wish. No sparkles. Not even the tiniest inkling of magic. Isabelle stared at her unopened books. No one had to tell her she wasn't ready for Level Two training.

If that wasn't bad enough, her sister, Clotilda, was the fourth best fairy godmother. Morning, noon, and night, she knocked on Isabelle's door and asked questions like: "Are you sure I can't help you with anything?" and "Why do you always have to make everything so difficult?" and the most obvious one, "You don't want to embarrass Grandmomma, do you?"

Grandmomma (with the emphasis on *grand*) was the president of the Fairy Godmother Alliance. She was also in charge of pretty much everything, from training to the Extravaganza to the creation of the rule book itself. She also happened to be Isabelle and Clotilda's *real* grand-mother so, no, Isabelle didn't want to embarrass her.

But, more than that, she didn't want to get in trouble, especially when Nora still had time to use the sparkles. The truth was, as long as there was still a sliver of hope that Nora might make a wish, Isabelle didn't want to be disturbed.

Clotilda was not giving up. "Isabelle," she said, banging on the door even harder. "What's the matter? I'm not the enemy. And I'm not going anywhere until you let me come in."

If Clotilda wanted to come in, Isabelle couldn't stop her.

So instead, Isabelle changed tactics. "Just a minute," she said, opening her *Official Rule Book for Fairy Godmothers, 11th Edition* and propping it up on her desk. She scattered a whole bunch of papers on top of her bed. If Isabelle could convince Clotilda she was studying, maybe her sister would leave.

Unfortunately, Clotilda knew an unread book when she saw one. "For pity's sake, this is worse than I expected!" She picked up Isabelle's brand-new glasses from the floor and cleaned off the smudges. Then she tapped her wand on every piece of furniture until the whole room sparkled. She didn't bother fixing Isabelle's unruly hair. (She was not a fairy godmother who enjoyed hopeless projects that didn't stand a chance of success.)

Clotilda opened the book to the section on Minimum Requirements for Advancement and told Isabelle to listen carefully. "To pass Level Two, you still need to be kind, determined, and full of gusto." (In other words, all of the above.) "But you will also need to acquire fortitude, resilience, and laser-beam focus!" When Isabelle flopped onto her bed, Clotilda said in her most twinkly and annoying voice, "Most of all, you have to stop moping around about Nora! I know you really liked her, but it just isn't practical for her to remember you!"

Isabelle hated Rule Three C. "So it didn't bother you that your first practice princess forgot you?"

"Of course it bothered me a little," Clotilda said. "But if you want to be a great fairy godmother, you have to deal with it. If it makes you feel better, your new princess— or regular girl—will deserve happily ever after, just like Nora did."

It sounded logical in theory, but it felt all wrong. "But what if I'm not ready?" Isabelle asked.

Clotilda reached into her pocket and pulled out a small but fat envelope made of gold-foil paper. "Don't worry, you don't have to thank me."

Isabelle tore open the package. She hoped she'd find something like dark chocolate with a coconut filling. Or maybe cinnamon cookies. But knowing Clotilda, it was probably something healthy, like dried fruit.

Or even more disappointing, a homemade card.

Across the front, it read: *For Isabelle: The Secret to My Success! Or: What you should have learned already, but probably haven't, and don't try to pretend you don't know what I'm talking about.*

(She was so annoying. And smart. Clotilda clearly knew Isabelle *still* hadn't read the rule book.)

Isabelle opened the cheat sheet. It was covered with glittery curlicues and hearts and stars—that was so Clotilda! Isabelle read:

Before you start Level Two, there are a few things you should remember:

a) Everyone deserves happily ever after. Your only job is to give it and go. Don't look back. No matter what it looks like, you really DO get the right princess at the right time. Every time! Not just the first time!

b) Don't take so long to get started! Dawdling makes everything harder. I shouldn't have to tell you, but sometimes happiness takes a while.

c) Simple wand work is the best! I am happy to help you if you have questions or want to practice!

d) Be nicer to Angelica and Fawn. They are the best in your class, and more important, they're just your age. Having friends is really important. Having friends who are great fairy godmothers is even better. You can help each other. But first, you must earn their respect. (You really don't want to be the worst!)

e) Please don't leave sparkles unattended. I shouldn't have to tell you that sparkles are our most precious resource. So be careful with them. We can't lose a single one!

When she was done reading, Isabelle tried to act cool, calm, and collected, but it was hard. If wasting one sparkle was bad, wasting a whole jar had to be grounds for immediate dismissal to the Fairy Godmother Home for Normal Girls. (That was the place where unsuccessful trainees were sent to do non-magical tasks.) It might even be bad enough for Grandmomma to banish her, just like she had banished Mom all those years ago.

Isabelle held her breath. She was willing to grovel and confess and beg for forgiveness. But Clotilda didn't want to talk about the Home or sparkles. She was concerned with Isabelle's signature style. "Take out your wand," she said. "Pretend I'm your princess and I just made a wish."

Isabelle was happy to comply. She loved flicking and swishing her wand and twirling in a circle before granting a wish.

Clotilda rolled her eyes. "Just as I suspected—it's way too fancy."

Isabelle was confused. "But I thought fancy was the best."

When Clotilda wagged her finger, she looked exactly like Grandmomma. "Fancy moves make fairy godmothers seem silly. If you want to be taken seriously, you have got to tone it down." She held out her own wand. "Listen to me. And try and do what I do."

First, Clotilda cut Isabelle's twirl out completely. Then she cut her swish in half.

Isabelle practiced in front of the mirror. "I think this looks boring."

"Well, I think you look like a pro."

Clotilda made Isabelle practice the whole thing twenty-five more times, until her half swish was as fast as lightning, her wand tap was snappier, and her style looked basically the same as Clotilda's.

"Now do yourself a favor and read the entire rule book," Clotilda said in the bossiest voice ever. "Forget about Nora. And get a good night's sleep. Level Two is hard for everyone. So please keep calm! And be ready for *anything*. Understand?"

When Isabelle said, "Understood," Clotilda (finally) left. Straightaway, Isabelle went to her secret hiding place, the cozy spot between the girlgoyles. But she wasn't going there to study. (She didn't even bother bringing her book.) First things first, she had to give Nora one last chance.

Isabelle looked up at the sky full of stars. She shouted, "Find the sparkles. Make a wish. I'm here. I'm your friend. I miss you."

When nothing happened, Isabelle counted to ten. Then she counted to twenty. Even when she promised the stars she wouldn't break any more rules or be annoyed by her sister—even when she promised to read every single rule five times—nothing happened.

It was time for Isabelle to face the facts: Her plan had failed. Isabelle had given away the jar full of magical, happiness-making sparkles (and risked everything she cared about) for absolutely nothing.

Nora had forgotten her. And now Isabelle needed to forget Nora.

Chapter Two

The Worst First Day Ever

It is hard to study when your heart hurts. But Isabelle tried.

She might not have opened the rule book or done any serious reading, but she did decorate Clotilda's cheat sheet with squares and diamonds. Then she practiced her new, boring signature style a few more times. And when that was done, she made a list of ways to befriend Angelica and Fawn and earn their respect. She also munched on some stale pretzels and leaned on the girlgoyles. More than any-thing, she really wanted some sympathy.

Unfortunately for Isabelle, the girlgoyles weren't all that into pity parties. In fact, if they had been able to talk, they would have told Isabelle that whining didn't equal work-ing. And being ready meant being rested. Also: They didn't appreciate the pretzel crumbs. Crumbs meant crows. Girlgoyles were not fond of them.

By the time Isabelle figured all this out herself, it was way too late for resting. It was that time of day when you could see the sun and the moon in the very same sky.

She hoped that was a good sign. She also hoped it was a good sign that neither Clotilda nor Grandmomma were at the breakfast table. As she walked down the path toward the Official Fairy Godmother Training Center, she wanted to believe that everything was a good sign—that Clotilda's "be ready for *anything*" was really *nothing*, and Angelica and Fawn would be over the moon (or at least somewhat pleased) to see her. Maybe Grandmomma would take it easy on all of them, or even better, spend the whole day bragging about the Bests and the power of sparkles. Then all Isabelle would have to do would be to sit there and look interested.

But when she arrived at the center, something was definitely wrong. Angelica, Fawn, and all of the Worsts—trainees who had failed and were going through retraining—sat on the grass. They were hunched over books and papers and they were writing. The doors weren't right, either. The sparkly door that used to have a sign on it that read, USE THIS DOOR IF YOU ARE READY TO BE A GREAT FAIRY GODMOTHER was boarded up. Instead, an even bigger sign was nailed over that one. It read, PLEASE TAKE ONE. An arrow pointed to a small box of papers next to the door. Next to that was a yellow-and-black safety can with a heavy lid marked PROPERTY OF THE BESTS. And PLEASE DEPOSIT ALL EXCESS SPARKLES HERE.

Since her wand was completely free of sparkles, Isabelle took a paper and waved at Angelica and Fawn, hoping they'd invite her to sit down. When they didn't wave back, she cleared her throat a few times, but that didn't get their attention, either. So instead, she asked in her friendliest voice, "What do you think's going on?"

"You think we know?" Angelica asked, fiddling with one of her long, thick braids. "She's your grandmother. We were hoping you could tell us."

Fawn crossed her arms and pouted. "I thought we were going to get to keep our extra sparkles."

This was not the start she was hoping for. Since Isabelle didn't want to talk about rules or excess sparkles, she sat down on the grass next to Minerva and the other Worsts, Irene and MaryEllen. Then she asked Minerva to borrow a pen. (She had forgotten hers.)

Minerva was the oldest and wrinkliest of the Worsts to go through retraining, and she was usually in a bad mood. Today was no exception. So Isabelle wasn't surprised when instead of saying hello, Minerva coughed like a cat with a hairball stuck in its throat.

"I don't like surprises," Minerva said.

Irene nodded. "Or giving away sparkles."

MaryEllen handed Isabelle a tissue. "Clean your glasses. They're filthy."

Isabelle's glasses (when they were clean) made the words on the page clearer, but they didn't make directions more interesting, especially when they were written in really long paragraphs and very small print. So Isabelle skipped those parts. Instead, she focused on the two big, bold lines in the middle of the page.

The Bests are grateful for your participation.

Please answer the following questions by circling "True" or "False."

It was a test! On Day One! That was so not nice! But at least the test was short. And it wasn't multiple choice. Isabelle didn't like those kinds of questions because there was always a trick, and she never caught on.

Isabelle looked at the questions and hoped they were easy.

True or False: I received enough sparkles during Level One to do my job.

True or False: I could not have done anything more with more sparkles.

True or False: I do not have any sparkles left in my possession at this time.

True or False: I have received no requests for extra sparkles.

True or False: The instructions regarding sparkles were clear.

True or False: I believe I am ready for Level Two—with or without sparkles.

Now Isabelle knew she was in trouble.

Six questions about sparkles had to mean one thing and one thing only: Grandmomma and the Bests knew about Nora.

She peeked at Minerva's test, just to see what she knew, too. Obviously, this was a dumb thing to do. But when you're nervous and scared and guilty of things that can get you banished, you make mistakes.

Minerva's handwriting was large and shaky. It was easy to read.

I exercise my right not to take this test. You gave us the minimal amount of sparkles. What is going on? Why was it necessary to put me in a class with children?

Isabelle felt bad for spying. She felt even worse when Minerva gave her a dirty look.

"If you hate it so much, why don't you just retire?" Isabelle asked.

"Because I like being a fairy godmother." Minerva put her paper away, limped to the door, and whistled so that the other trainees would look at her. "I know all of you think you're ready to be great fairy godmothers, but apparently, the Bests don't agree." She held open the brown NOT READY door. "Anyone coming with me?"

Irene and MaryEllen got up first and walked slowly

through the open door. Once it was clear that nothing bad would happen, Fawn glided in. Isabelle wanted to go next, but Angelica beat her to it. She leapt over the threshold the way Nora used to when she didn't want to step on a crack in the sidewalk. So Isabelle did that, too, just in case there was something to it.

Inside the training center, a lot of things looked the same.

There were still rows of chairs and desks. And Grandmomma's huge jar of candy was filled to the brim. Her big, red chair was still big and red and scary. Isabelle's favorite sign, HAPPY EVER AFTER. THE LAST LINE OF EVERY GREAT STORY, still hung behind the desk, though today it was a little bit crooked.

A lot of things looked different.

For example, the Level Two slogans on the back wall. Isabelle wasn't sure about DON'T DREAM OF SUCCESS— WORK FOR IT! or USE YOUR HEART AND YOUR HEAD. But she liked KEEP CALM AND SPARKLE ON! (She was pretty sure

Clotilda had written it. It sounded just like something her sister would say.)

Next to the slogans, new photos from the most recent Extravaganza, mostly of the top three ranking fairy godmothers—Luciana, Raine, and Kaminari—hung on the wall. In one, Luciana accepted a large bouquet of orange, black, and yellow wildflowers from Raine. In another, Kaminari led a small group of godmothers in what looked to be the cha-cha. But maybe it was another dance.

There were also a bunch of group pictures. In the middle was a big one of Angelica and Fawn with Clotilda, their arms linked and big smiles on their faces.

"You know, you should have been in this one, too," Angelica said. Isabelle couldn't tell if she was disappointed or cross. "We looked all over for you. Your sister was really upset."

Isabelle didn't like being left out, but there was no way she could tell Angelica or Fawn the truth about where she had been (or about leaving the sparkles for Nora). So she said, "I'm so disappointed! I think I was standing on the balcony. It was such a beautiful night. Don't you remember?" She hoped they bought her excuse.

Isabelle turned her attention to the other pictures. There was a great one of Grandmomma, and a funny one of Minerva and the other Worsts. They had red icing on their teeth. Angelica and Fawn couldn't help but laugh.

Isabelle was just about to point out another funny picture (and hopefully get them to like her) when the door swung open. All the lights turned turquoise blue.

"Grandmomma?" Isabelle said.

But instead of Grandmomma, Luciana the *Fascinante* sauntered into the room, her wand pointed up and away (for safety) and her skirts swishing with every step she took toward Grandmomma's chair and desk. Luciana was called Luciana the *Fascinante* because that's what her first princess called her. She was also the Number One fairy godmother in the world, or in other words, the best of the Bests. So no one was going to argue about her name.

Angelica dashed to the front of the room. *"¡Qué gran sorpresa!"* she said with a curtsy. (That means: "What a nice surprise!" in Spanish.)

Luciana curtsied back. *"Gracias, arigato,* and *todah!"* (That means "thank you" in a bunch of languages.)

She hopped up on Grandmomma's desk and flicked her wand to restore the lights. Then she picked up an official rule book and flipped through the pages. "Take a seat," she said. "Welcome to Level Two. As you might have already surmised, things are going to be a little different this term."

Chapter Three

Under the Circumstances

*D*ifferent was one thing. But if you asked Isabelle (and nobody did), training without Grandmomma felt completely wrong.

Unlike Grandmomma, who enjoyed pondering the honorable life of being a fairy godmother, Luciana didn't mention the joys of making someone happily ever after or the importance of testing or how the bond between a fairy godmother and a princess was a sacred thing that they would always cherish. She didn't review any of the rules or repeat any of Grandmomma's favorites, like: "There is no such thing as a lousy princess." And "You always get the right princess at the right time."

Mostly Luciana talked about the importance of conserving sparkles. And that under the circumstances, things were going to be a little different for trainees and their practice princesses. Also harder. And that under the circumstances, that was okay with her because she thought that training had become way too easy anyway.

All this "under the circumstances" made Isabelle even jumpier than she already was. She wished Luciana would get it over with and spell out what the circumstances actually were. Or that Grandmomma would show up— even if that meant Isabelle getting in trouble. Luciana talked too fast. And she only talked about practice princesses and never included regular girls like Nora.

But Isabelle knew better than to complain to Luciana the *Fascinante*.

So to stay calm (and awake), Isabelle drew squares all

over her paper, and then by accident, she doodled right on her desk. Even though Isabelle knew it wasn't polite to draw on furniture, she couldn't help it. The wood of the desk was old and soft, and pushing her pencil into it was really satisfying. Isabelle also clearly wasn't the first to do this. Her desk was already covered with tiny carvings from past trainees.

She was just about to carve a brand-new square (or maybe a triangle) when a shadow fell across her desk and she felt a perfectly manicured hand on her shoulder. Isabelle did not have to look up to know that this hand belonged to Luciana, and that she had officially been caught writing on the furniture.

With one flick of the wand, Luciana turned Isabelle's doodle into a bright red, shiny apple. It was so shiny it looked like it could hold magic. Luciana ate the whole thing, bite by bite, and tossed the core in the trash. "Before we begin today's training, I would like to speak to each one of you. One by one. Best to worst."

Fawn must have known she was best in the class, because she stood up right away. Physically, Fawn still reminded Isabelle of a cloud, but she no longer looked like she was going to blow away. As Luciana waved her wand all around the girl, Fawn looked solid. And strong. And confident.

Luciana asked three questions: "Did you enjoy being a fairy godmother?" and "What was the easiest part?" and "What was hardest?"

Fawn glowed tawny pink—like a cloud right before sunset.

"The best part was the feeling of making my princess happily ever after," Fawn said. Then she thanked Luciana profusely and told her how much fun it had been to delight her practice princess with a surprise sprinkling of soft, white, glistening snow. "It wasn't hard at all! There's nothing more enjoyable than granting a wish."

Isabelle didn't think they were supposed to brag. Also, she hadn't found getting to *happily ever after* easy at all.

To be honest, listening hadn't been that enjoyable. It was a lot like waiting. Which meant it was mostly boring.

When Fawn sat down, Angelica stood up. She seemed stronger and more confident, too. She had woven shiny, red ribbon into her braids and dyed the tips a deep purple.

Like Fawn, Angelica had also loved listening and making her princess H.E.A., which was her new snappy way of saying *happily ever after*. She made a big point of adding how really, *really* grateful she was to have been given a princess with an adventurous streak, since according to her, adventurous princesses were the best. Before walking back to her seat, she added that nothing was hard. "I found the whole process very easy. I returned almost half a teaspoon of sparkles back to the can."

Luciana said something in another language. Isabelle was sure it meant: "You, my dear, are more impressive than your friend, and I know next time you will be Number One in the class."

Isabelle hoped her name would be called next. But it wasn't. Minerva's was. But Minerva wasn't about to get up. "What's going on with the sparkles?" she asked from the back row. "And where's Elizabeth Marie?"

No one called Grandmomma Elizabeth Marie. Not to her face. Or even behind her back.

Isabelle slunk low in her seat as Luciana strutted to the back of the room. Isabelle was sure Minerva was about to be expelled. But instead, Luciana asked her, Irene, and MaryEllen the same questions she asked Fawn and Angelica. Then she asked Isabelle to join her at the front of the room.

Standing this close to the number one ranking fairy godmother was nothing less than terrifying. Luciana had piercing eyes and arched eyebrows and very sharp, pointy maroon fingernails with rhinestones on all of the tips. Her clothes made Isabelle feel like sneezing—they smelled like basil, mint, and fresh green pepper. And her wand was extremely long. When she flicked it, it made Isabelle's fingers and toes feel tingly and her heart feel happy—sort of like wings fluttering. Or leaves swishing in the wind.

Isabelle took a step back. She was sure the wand had the power to shock her. Or make her confess.

(For the record, fairy godmother magic doesn't work that way. It never makes anyone do anything unless it's something that person *wants* to do. So Isabelle didn't have to worry about that.)

"We're all very curious," the Number One fairy godmother said, waving her wand very close to Isabelle's face. "Did you enjoy working with your regular girl?"

"I enjoyed it immensely," Isabelle said, taking a tiny step back. "We cleaned up the world. We made posters. We became friends."

She heard someone snicker. It was probably Angelica. Or maybe it was Fawn.

"Did you face any challenges?"

"Yes," Isabelle replied very seriously. "Nora didn't think

fairy godmothers were real. So at first, she made really big wishes."

When Luciana said, "That *would* be a problem," everyone laughed.

Isabelle didn't like how they were looking at her—or laughing at Nora. "I might have needed every last second—and sparkle—to get her to happily ever after, but it was worth it. Nora might be a regular girl, but she was as great as any practice princess. Maybe even greater."

Then, as fast as she could, she scrambled back to her seat.

Luciana waved her wand East, South, West, and North. "Thank you all for your honesty. Now I want to be honest, too, and prepare you for what comes next. In Level Two, training is always more challenging. But under the circumstances, it's going to be even tougher."

Isabelle wiggled in her seat. Granting wishes and making a practice princess (or regular girl) happily ever after was hard enough. Why did it have to become tougher?

She had a feeling she was about to find out.

Luciana told all the trainees to face the back door. "To help us with our work, let's welcome the second, third, and fourth best fairy godmothers. And an extra special guest, too."

Isabelle turned to face the back.

She crossed her fingers.

She hoped that the special guest was Grandmomma.

It just had to be her.

Chapter Four

The Oldest Godmother Ever

Trumpets blared. The lights flickered. The back door flew open. Everyone applauded. Partly because it was always exciting to see the Bests. But also because it was the first thing all day that felt even a teensy bit normal.

Raine—the second best godmother—looked majestic in a copper gown with wide flowing sleeves, decorated with shimmering metallic fringe. The third best god-mother, Kaminari, was wearing clothes that were trim and tailored. But when the light hit her hair and clothes—wow! She shimmered like liquid glass.

But when Clotilda walked in wearing a sparkly tiara and old-fashioned fairy godmother clothes, everyone burst into giggles. These were the kind of impractical clothes you found in books but that modern fairy godmothers never wore. Her dress had big puffy sleeves, and her long tulle skirt kept snagging on all the desks.

"Why are you wearing that?" Isabelle asked. Clotilda was not the kind of fairy godmother to make such silly mistakes with clothes.

"Obviously," Clotilda said, trying not to look miffed, "Raine and Kaminari played a joke on me." She tugged at a satin ribbon. "They told me it was dress-up day. Their magic is stronger than mine."

Everyone gathered around Clotilda to check out her custom glass shoes. That is, until the back door blew open with a scorching-hot gust of air. It was the special guest. They'd forgotten all about her.

(Unfortunately, it wasn't Grandmomma.)

Instead, a very old fairy godmother—the oldest Isabelle had ever seen—hobbled into the room. She walked with a cane. She kept her wand tucked behind her ear.

This godmother was shorter than Kaminari and more stooped than Minerva. Her olive skin was so wrinkly and worn she looked old enough to have been the first fairy godmother of all time.

"Zahara!" Minerva shouted.

As fast as she could (in other words, faster than usual, but still really slowly), she limped to the antique godmother. They embraced like old friends.

"I don't believe it," Minerva said at least three times. "I thought you were . . ."

"Dead?"

Even though it could have been an awkward moment, the two old godmothers burst into fits of croaky laughter. So did Irene and MaryEllen, who apparently had also thought Zahara was dead. Even Luciana looked amused.

While Raine and Kaminari helped her to Grandmomma's chair, Clotilda didn't move a muscle. She stood in the corner with her arms crossed and a frown on her face.

This little act of defiance had nothing to do with her dress—she was over that. She frowned because Zahara wasn't some random ancient fairy godmother. She was the ancient fairy godmother who used to be Grandmomma's best friend, with the emphasis on *used to be*. Isabelle didn't remember ever meeting the old fairy godmother, but she'd never forget the last time some old godmother mentioned Zahara's name around her grandmother.

It was not a nice memory. It was not fun to see your grandmomma cry.

And now Grandmomma was *nowhere to be found* and Zahara was getting comfortable in her chair and acting like this was totally normal. But it wasn't normal. Or fair. Or nice. Just like everything else, this probably had to do with sparkles. So Isabelle just sat there and tried not to draw attention to herself.

For the first time since Level One began, the Worsts could not have looked happier. They scooted their seats toward the front of the room.

"Where have you been all this time?" Minerva asked. (Isabelle was sort of curious about that, too.)

"My so-called demise was obviously a rumor," Zahara said. "The truth is, I retired. But after a while, it got boring. So when Luciana called, I un-retired."

"When I was a young godmother, Zahara was famous for taking all the hardest-to-please princesses—even the ones who seemed destined for unhappily ever after," Minerva told Angelica, Fawn, and Isabelle. "If there had been training back then, I would have given anything to take a class with her."

Zahara popped the lid off Grandmomma's candy jar and took three peppermint patties (Grandmomma's favorite). She tossed them all in her mouth, closed her eyes, and leaned back in her chair. Then her mouth fell open. She began to snore.

Luciana sent a few lightning sprays through the room, and everyone (including Zahara) bolted up in their chairs.

"Zahara, can you tell the trainees about the kinds of princesses you helped over the years?" Luciana asked.

"Well, there was the one who fell in love with the handsome prince who had a curse on his head," Zahara began. "That poor girl was the very definition of fortitude. First she saved him from drowning. Then she rescued him from an alligator. Before he was in the clear, she had to save him from his own dog."

"I read about her," Angelica said. "But I don't understand: Why didn't you just remove the curse? Wouldn't that have been a lot faster?"

"In the old days, we didn't care so much about speed," Zahara said. "Back then, it was much more important to test our princesses and see if they had the strength to be happily ever after . . . or if they didn't."

Everyone gasped. Since the whole thing with Mom, getting to happily ever after (or as Angelica would say, H.E.A.) as quickly as possible was pretty much the whole point to training—at least Isabelle thought that was the point.

Maybe Zahara had been *asked* to retire. Maybe that's why she and Grandmomma weren't friends anymore. Isabelle raised her hand. "You don't need to teach us anything about independence. Grandmomma taught us that in Level One." (She was feeling very defensive of Grandmomma.)

At the mention of Grandmomma, Zahara didn't even flinch. "Hello, Isabelle. The last time I saw you, I believe you were toddling around the castle. You were so cute. I see your hair hasn't changed a bit."

It was always annoying when adults said things like that.

"As for independence," Zahara said, "or what I would call *patience and fortitude and common sense*, let me tell you about my first princess, a young *ameerah* named Noni, her sister, a king, and a pair of golden slippers."

There wasn't a fairy godmother who didn't love a good shoe story. Fawn opened her Wish List to a page at the beginning of the book (where Noni's story was printed). "Before you tell us the details, would you sign my Wish List?" she gushed, and giggled. "Noni's story is one of my favorites."

After signing Fawn's Wish List and then Angelica's, Zahara leaned back in her chair and started the story. "As some of you may already know, Noni was a poor girl who lived near a beautiful, winding river with her mean older sister. This sister was very jealous of Noni's kindness and beauty and her one possession, a pair of lovely gold shoes."

Angelica raised her hand. "The shoes were from her father, right?"

Zahara smiled. "The shoes always come from someone who loves you." For the first time, Isabelle realized Zahara was missing two teeth. "When her sister received an invitation to meet the king, Noni asked to come along, but her sister forbade it. Probably because she knew the king would like Noni the best."

Isabelle could totally relate to the whole sister problem. What she didn't understand was Zahara. "So why didn't you tell the king to have a party?" (She was pretty sure that was how Clotilda would do it.)

Luciana looked a little annoyed. "Because obviously Noni had chores to do."

Isabelle forgot how much fairy godmothers used to love making princesses do chores. But she also never really got why they were so important.

Before she could raise her hand and ask, Zahara explained that chores made Noni a humble princess. They also gave her time. And when she said *time*, she meant time to become stronger and wiser. "When Noni had worked so long and so hard her feet finally couldn't take it another day, she took off her shoes and went for a swim. She made a sincere and selfless wish for happiness. That was my cue. I turned myself into an eagle, swiped one of the shoes, and gave it to the king. He didn't need a party because back then, kings knew that eagles meant power and happiness."

"And the rest was easy peasy, lemon squeezy," Fawn and Angelica said together.

Zahara nodded. "Without requiring another sparkle, the shoe led the king on a long search for its owner. Eventually, he arrived at the lovely girl's home. By then, she had done even more chores and become very wise. So when they met, she was ready to be queen. They fell in love and lived happily ever after."

It was hard holding a grudge when the stories were this mushy. But Isabelle still didn't get it. "How can a wish be selfless? Won't princesses complain if we make them work too hard?"

Zahara popped out of her chair. "Haven't you heard a word I said? In today's world, our princesses need to be strong. And smart. And powerful. They need a chance to show us what they're made of."

When everyone started talking at once, Luciana raised her wand. "Trainees, now you know why we invited Zahara to join us for Level Two training. We are going to ask you not just to be sweet and nice and full of gusto, but also brilliant and gritty and more determined than you ever imagined. Happily ever after will always be the last line of every great story, but it's rarely easy to attain! That's why, in Level Two, your tasks will be complicated. And so will your princesses!"

When she put down her wand, Isabelle hoped that meant a break. She wanted to go home and talk to Grandmomma. She had a million questions. Plus she was exhausted.

But it wasn't time to take a break—not by a long shot.

It was time for official training to begin.

Chapter Five

The Very Long First Day and Night, Part One

To warm up, Raine asked the trainees to run around a bunch of cones (to test their endurance). Then Kaminari led them in a ballet class (to teach them grace). These were the same tasks they'd done in Level One, but this time, they ran while carrying stacks of old editions of the *Official Rule Book for Fairy Godmothers*. They practiced ballet on ice.

In other words, it was a lot harder.

When they were done, they were not allowed to rest. Instead, Zahara told them to stand close together. She wanted them to do something new. She called it a human knot.

"With your right hand, find someone's hand and hold tight," Zahara instructed them.

Then they all had to do the same thing with their left hands. And then they had to untangle themselves. It wasn't easy. Someone smelled funny (probably Isabelle—since she hadn't had time to shower). And Minerva kept stepping on Isabelle's foot.

When they were done, Zahara asked them what they had learned.

Angelica raised her hand first. "To work together."

"And to listen," Fawn added. "Because we know that's always the first step toward happily ever after."

Zahara yawned, like those were the most boring answers ever.

"What about you, Isabelle?" she asked. "What did you learn?"

Isabelle remembered all the things she'd learned from Nora. "I learned that there is always a way out, even when it looks hopeless. And that you just have to keep trying and maybe also give up a little bit so that you can get where you want to go."

For a moment, no one said anything. (It wasn't every day that Isabelle answered a question correctly.)

"I guess I understand mistakes better than the rest of you!" Isabelle said with a shrug.

When Zahara had stopped laughing, she gave Isabelle a piece of dark chocolate with a cherry inside. (It was delicious.) Then she pointed to the window so everyone could see it was getting dark. As Zahara explained, this meant things were about to get "interesting."

The Worsts chuckled. Isabelle yawned. She was really tired.

"What do you mean, interesting?" she asked.

Zahara asked them to turn to Section Six of the rule book on the advantages of granting wishes in the dark.

"In the history of fairy godmothers and their princesses, a lot of great magic is made when no one can see what you're doing," she said with a crooked smile.

When they were done reading the entire chapter, Luciana flicked her wand and six large crates appeared— one for each trainee.

"That's why your first big assignment will be tonight," Luciana explained.

Isabelle raised her hand. "Are we going to get some sparkles?"

"One sparkle," Kaminari said. "We want to see what you can do in the garden."

This was a big letdown, until Raine reminded them that gardens, like the woods and other natural habitats, were fruitful (pun intended) settings for wish fulfillment. Raine also explained that many fairy godmothers are gardeners because, in a pinch, flowers, fruits, and vegetables could be used in a variety of wishes and charms.

Kaminari gave each trainee a handful of mismatched seeds and a small velvet bag.

Inside the bag was a strange-looking sparkle. To be honest, it was actually really ugly compared to regular sparkles. It was gray and not very sparkly, like a misshapen piece of salt.

"This sparkle isn't just any sparkle," Luciana told the trainees. "It's a raw sparkle. You should be honored!" According to Clotilda, raw sparkles were as powerful as the refined sparkles fairy godmothers usually worked with, but they were unprocessed. (Later, Minerva would tell Isabelle this wasn't exactly true. She thought raw sparkles were sparkles that had been discarded. Grade Two. Maybe even recalled. In other words, they weren't as good. But Isabelle had no idea who was right.)

But for now, the trainees all smiled. Kaminari assigned them each a crate full of tools. Then she told them that in the morning, the Bests and Zahara would return to see what each trainee had done.

"But what are we supposed to do?" Isabelle said. The official gardens were at least two miles away. And those crates looked heavy. She looked at her handful of seeds. She couldn't tell if they were fruits or flowers or weeds.

Angelica rolled her eyes. "I think the whole point is to figure it out ourselves."

Luciana agreed. "Angelica is right." She gave Angelica a hunk of chocolate laced with caramel. Then all the Bests walked out the door and the trainees got to work.

First things first. Isabelle picked up the box of tools, and as she suspected, it was both heavy and clunky. She thought about using her sparkle to transport herself and everything else to the garden, but that seemed lazy. Besides, no one else was doing that. They all looked busy. Like they knew just what to do.

So she put the seeds and the sparkle in her backpack, picked up the crate, and started walking to the garden.

No sooner had Isabelle left than it began to rain. It wasn't just a light drizzle, either—this was the kind of rain that often happens when a witch or mean sister wants to make things tough on a princess. In other words, it was a cold, hard rain. With wind and an occasional bolt of lightning. As Isabelle walked through some trees and down a dirt path and up a few small hills to the Official Fairy Godmother Garden, she became more and more miserable. A few times, she slipped and fell. She skinned both her knees. She dropped a few seeds. To be honest, she was a little bit scared. Her crate began to fall apart. She couldn't see where she was going. Her glasses were useless!

Even worse, by the time Isabelle got there, all the other trainees were already there, and they didn't look tired or wet or scared. In fact, Fawn and Angelica seemed to be finishing up, and they were working under what looked like a giant yellow-and-white umbrella that glowed and protected them like their very own sun. The Worsts looked almost done, too (although their umbrella was plain). Isabelle met Minerva at a scarecrow in an old-fashioned red ball gown—her design. "How did everyone get here so fast?"

"The three of us decided to work together," Minerva said a little sheepishly. "So I used my sparkle for travel— and this gal." She patted the scarecrow on the shoulder. "Irene is using hers for planting. And MaryEllen made the umbrella." She gave Isabelle's shoulder a quick squeeze. "Don't be mad. It was the only way. We're too old for all this walking."

Isabelle wasn't mad, but she did feel left out. Working together had been a good idea. It was obviously what Angelica and Fawn were doing, too. Without her. On purpose.

Minerva said, "You know, if you run into trouble, break your sparkle in half. They're so brittle, you can crack them with your teeth. You want to try it?"

Isabelle shook her head no. "Not now. No thanks." She didn't want help. She didn't want apologies. Instead, she sat down and waited until all of them were gone. Then she looked up at the sky. For a moment, through the clouds, she could see one bright, twinkling star.

For that moment, it felt like she wasn't alone. It felt like someone was watching. Maybe even her mother.

Very quickly, Isabelle dug a hole and threw the few seeds she could find into it. And then, because she didn't know what else to do, she threw the sparkle in, too. Then she lay on the ground and watched that star twinkle until accidentally, she fell asleep.

Chapter Six

The Very Long First Day and Night,
Part Two

When Isabelle woke up, the sun was bright. Angelica, Fawn, the Worsts, and the Bests all stood over her.

"Good morning, sleepyhead," they shouted together.

Isabelle stood up and brushed herself off. Then she turned around. She couldn't believe what the sparkles had done to the garden.

In one corner, next to the overdressed scarecrow, there was a perfectly round rosebush with one perfect, thorny rose peeking up through the top. In the other corner, there was a star-shaped plot of exotic plants and blossoms. And in the middle of the garden stood a gigantic, gnarly tree covered with pink blossoms.

It was the kind of gigantic, gnarly tree that often shows up in magical stories—the kind that sometimes comes to life.

When the wind blew, the blossoms gently fell to the ground. They looked like one of Clotilda's skirts—beautiful and colorful and just plain princess-ready.

"That is amazing," Isabelle told Angelica. She assumed the tree was Angelica's creation. She also assumed that Angelica, like Clotilda, liked flattery.

But apparently she didn't.

"Why are you trying to embarrass me?" Angelica said. Then the shocker: "You know that tree isn't mine."

Isabelle was confused. "But if it isn't yours, whose is it?"

Clotilda jabbed Isabelle in the side, then gave her a big hug.

"Wait a minute," Isabelle said. "It's mine?"

Luciana, Raine, and Kaminari congratulated Isabelle.

"When did you decide to bury your sparkle?" Raine asked.

Isabelle stood there in disbelief. Angelica rolled her eyes. Then she whispered loudly to Fawn so everyone could hear, "I bet she dropped that sparkle in the hole by mistake." She told Luciana, "She didn't even know she could break it in half."

Isabelle hung her head and stared at the pink petals that skimmed the ground thanks to a light breeze. This was not going well at all. She was pretty sure Angelica and Fawn were never going to be her friends.

Clotilda gave her an encouraging smile. "Why don't you tell us what you did?"

"Angelica's right," Isabelle said. "I didn't know I could work in groups. I didn't know I could break the sparkle in half. By the time I got here, it was late and I was tired, and

I was 99.9 percent sure I was going to fail. So I threw the sparkle in the hole. Honestly, I didn't know what else to do. The other gardens are so much better."

She waited for Luciana to declare her the worst. But instead, Zahara clapped her hands. "Your choices may not have been the savviest, but you followed through with fortitude. And that's why you get first prize. Keep this up, Isabelle. If you do, you'll become a fine fairy godmother."

Isabelle should have felt great. She should have smiled and said thank you. But the truth was, she felt sad. A gnarly tree was pretty amazing, but it had been a complete mistake! Plus, Angelica looked furious. And Fawn seemed annoyed. All the way back to the center, they ranted about luck and the law of averages and the power of a whole raw sparkle. In their opinion, Isabelle was here because of Clotilda and Grandmomma. She didn't think things through. Even the worst fairy godmother got lucky once in a while.

By the time they returned to the center, Isabelle's confidence was shot. She hoped Luciana would let them go home. She wanted to go back to see the girlgoyles. And talk it out with Clotilda. And she really wanted to take a nap.

But Luciana had more for the trainees to do. "For your next task, you'll work in teams." She paired Minerva and Fawn with Kaminari, Irene and MaryEllen with Clotilda, and Angelica and Isabelle with Raine.

Raine placed a rose hip and four tiny raw sparkles in front of Angelica and Isabelle. The sparkles were the size of flecks of dust. They looked like they'd gone through a grinder.

Raine told them, "Work together to make your rose grow as tall and as straight as possible."

Angelica picked up the hip. She had perfect posture, like the tallest, strongest tree. "Are you sure you can do this?" she asked Isabelle in a way that said she didn't think Isabelle could.

Isabelle knew this was her chance to prove she could be a good friend. "Actually, I'm sort of tired. Why don't you take three sparkles, since you're so much stronger than me. Then we'll be the best. Luciana will be impressed. I promise, I'll give you all the credit." Isabelle was sure that if they were the best, Angelica and Fawn would forgive her. And maybe even like her more.

Fawn and Minerva went first. They stood up together, arms linked, wands pointed toward their hip. Together they tap, tap, tapped their wands in perfect unison. And right away, a rose bloomed. Kaminari held it to her nose. "Lovely," she said. "And only three thorns."

Irene and MaryEllen also linked arms, but they stayed seated. Tap, tap, tap! Their rose didn't grow quite as tall or straight as Fawn and Minerva's, but it was a little bit redder and grew only two thorns. Clotilda was particularly impressed. "Good concentration. You ladies are really feeling it."

Last, it was Isabelle and Angelica's turn. They stood up together, but when Isabelle tried to link arms with Angelica, her arms stayed stiff. When she held up her wand, Angelica whispered, "Don't mess this up. Or else!"

Threats like that only make fairy godmothers (and regular people) nervous.

In other words, Isabelle messed everything up.

First she dropped her wand. Then she held the wrong end up. When she said she was ready, she really wasn't.

Tap, tap, tap. Angelica's wand was faster than lightning. Isabelle's wasn't quite that fast, so her taps lagged a half a tap behind. Isabelle hoped it didn't matter. She hoped their red rose would be perfect and then they could all go home and maybe she could invite Angelica and Fawn to the castle for cupcakes, since it was a proven fact of fairy godmother life that snacks sealed friendships faster than anything else.

At first, the rose grew like all the others. Straight and

strong. A thorn here and there. But when the petals began to bloom, they were too heavy. They drooped immediately. One petal even looked a little brown near the edges.

Raine plucked the dying petal off to make the rose look better. She examined it from all angles. "On the plus side, it's very mature."

Isabelle knew that there was no plus side to *mature. Very mature* was just a nice way of saying *old* or *stale* or *unacceptable* or *bad.* Isabelle took the blame. "It's my fault, Raine. Sorry, Angelica. My wand work is too slow."

Isabelle hoped Angelica would accept her apology, but instead, she threw Isabelle under the bus. "It was more than her wand speed," Angelica said meanly. "Isabelle insisted I use most of the sparkles. It was really hard to work with her."

Now everyone was looking at Isabelle and shaking their heads, as if she had made Angelica fail on purpose.

"Can Angelica try it one more time?" Isabelle asked Luciana. She was willing to beg if she had to. "Without me?"

Luciana looked angry. "No, she can't try it again because that would be wasting sparkles. And under the circumstances, we are not going to do that." Then she dismissed the group and puff—disappeared in a cloud of sparkle dust.

Raine walked to the front of the room. "Well, you heard Luciana. See you tomorrow."

After the Bests were gone, Angelica and Fawn packed up their stuff and strutted toward the door. "Wait!" Isabelle said.

Fawn turned around. "For you? No thank you." She linked arms with Angelica and they walked out the door, noses and wands high (even though their wands didn't hold any sparkles).

Isabelle flopped down into her chair. She put her head on her desk and let the Worsts console her.

Minerva assured Isabelle that the day hadn't been a complete disaster. "What about that tree? You did a great job with that."

Irene and MaryEllen agreed. "And your rose was quite nice, too."

Isabelle was pretty sure the rose had been a total disaster. "Angelica and Fawn didn't think so," she said. "And please don't tell me Angelica's jealous—or that she must be hurting, too." (In the fairy godmother world, like the regular one, the regular excuses rarely felt authentic.)

So the Worsts said other unhelpful things like, "Tomorrow's a new day," and "Nothing is set in stone," and "We're all under a great deal of pressure."

"Why don't you go home and talk to your grand-momma?" Minerva said. "I heard she isn't leaving until tomorrow. I'm sure she'll know exactly what to do."

Chapter Seven

The Problem with Responsibilities

Leaving? Isabelle's face flushed. Her whole body felt hot and cold at once. Where was Grandmomma going? And why?

Isabelle ran back to the castle as fast as she could. It was bad enough that her mother wasn't here. Grandmomma couldn't leave, too.

Isabelle didn't even bother to take off her dirty shoes before she ran up the stairs and across the red rug to the end of the hall. Without hesitating, she banged on the brass lion knocker on Grandmomma's office door. The lion looked like it was growling at her. Like she was way too late. Or like it didn't want to be disturbed.

But Isabelle didn't know what else to do or where else to look, so she knocked again. And then again.

"I promise I'll read the rule book," she shouted. "And I'll never embarrass you again." She kept at it, yelling and banging and making promises that she couldn't guarantee, until she felt a cold, bony hand touch her shoulder.

It was Grandmomma. She was wearing a plush pink-and-lavender bathrobe (complete with gold trim around the edges) and a white-and-pink shower cap. "I heard you made a very beautiful tree."

This was the best compliment Grandmomma had ever given her.

"Did they also tell you I fell asleep?" Isabelle asked.

"They didn't have to." Grandmomma pulled a twig out of Isabelle's hair. Grandmomma had a magic spyglass.

She used it to watch things that were happening all over the fairy godmother world.

"I presume you'd like to talk?" Grandmomma asked Isabelle as she held open the door to her office.

Grandmomma's office was filled with all kinds of fairy godmother bling, including photos of past princesses and godmothers, shoes, and a spinning wheel. Isabelle tried avoiding the vintage mirror, but to no avail. (It was hard not to look.) And when she did peek, Isabelle saw that her hair was worse than ever, and that there were still a few twigs and leaves stuck to her dress.

She also saw a suitcase, and it looked packed. Ready to go.

"Where are you going?" Isabelle asked, without a tremor in her voice, even though she was very nervous she wasn't going to like the answer.

Grandmomma looked very stern and serious. "If you ever become a great fairy godmother in charge of Official Training, the rule book, and much of the fairy godmother world, you will understand that sometimes you can't be everywhere at once."

Isabelle was 99.9 percent sure she would never be in charge of anything, but she didn't say that. "You can't send Luciana?"

Grandmomma shook her head. "No. I can't. This matter is too important." She looked very serious—even more so than usual. "Isabelle, why don't you let me worry about my job and you worry about yours. Focus on your studies. Luciana and the Bests will do a great job in Level Two."

"Well, they're not," Isabelle said. "Luciana hardly gives us any sparkles. She and the Bests made us work in teams. She brought back Zahara. And she let her sit in your chair."

Grandmomma winced for a second. "I brought back Zahara," she said. "I thought you, in particular, would benefit from her experience."

"But then why is Luciana being so stingy with the sparkles? Why does she keep saying 'under the circumstances' like something terrible is happening?"

Grandmomma took off her shower cap, wiggled out of her slippers, and sat down behind her desk. "Isabelle, can I trust you with some very important information?"

Isabelle nodded. She said absolutely nothing.

"Recently, I began to notice some slight irregularities in the world of princesses and in our overall inventory of sparkles."

Isabelle tried not to look nervous. She said absolutely nothing at all.

"At first, it didn't seem that terrible," Grandmomma said. "Maybe it was even a coincidence. One princess tripping while making a grand entrance is never cause for alarm. But then another was late for an important date—right after making a wish. And another very smart princess insulted an entire nation for absolutely no reason at all. And then Melody took a bad spill."

"Is she all right?" Isabelle asked. Melody was Clotilda's princess. As far as Isabelle knew, she was nearly happily ever after.

"Just a little shook up. Nothing she can't handle."
Grandmomma paused. She looked into Isabelle's eyes. "I
don't need to explain to you that the happiness of the fairy
godmother world relies on the happiness of the princess
world. And that we can't take any chances with shenanigans like this. When sparkles are being made to make
mischief, things can get out of hand very fast. We don't
want anything bad to happen. To the princesses. Or the
practice princesses. Or any of you."

Isabelle was too young to remember the time when the
unhappy princess gave up being a princess (and Mom
had been banished). But she knew she didn't want to go
back to that time, even though she missed Mom. "You're
sure sparkles are involved? And that you have to go?"

Grandmomma stood over Isabelle and told her that
she'd have to trust her on that—and other things.
"Isabelle, Luciana is an excellent teacher. She may not test
you the way I tested you, but she will want to see that
you have the best interests of our princesses in your heart.

And Zahara can teach you a lot about accessories. I'm sure all of you will enjoy that."

Isabelle definitely wanted to learn about accessories. But she was more worried about Nora's sparkles—and the possibility that they had fallen into the wrong hands. She was also worried about Grandmomma. And if she was being honest, she was nervous for herself, too. "And you're definitely coming back?"

"As soon as everything is settled, I'll be back in my chair." Even though she wasn't the hugging type, she gave Isabelle a quick squeeze. "Right now, the best thing you can do is work hard. Pass your training. Make me proud. If you have concerns, talk to your sister. I promise you—I will be fine."

When fairy godmothers (and regular people) say that they will be fine, it usually means that something isn't quite as fine as the word might imply. So it usually doesn't make the person who asked feel any better about things.

But in this case, fine would have to do. Grandmomma

was not going to say anything more. So Isabelle went to her room, gathered some blankets, and headed to the girlgoyles. There, she set up a tent between them, even though the girlgoyles still hadn't changed their minds about pity parties.

But for the first time, Isabelle didn't just feel alone. She felt lonely. There was a difference.

She wished the girlgoyles were real friends rather than statues. She wished that Angelica and Fawn—but especially Angelica—didn't look at her like she was always about to mess up. She wished that she could talk to Nora. (And that the sparkles were still safe in her memory box.)

More than anything, she wished she could talk to Mom. She wished with all her heart that Mom wasn't the one causing problems.

The problem was, Isabelle was a fairy godmother. Not a princess. And a fairy godmother's wishes never came true.

Chapter Eight

Necklaces, Shoes, and Other Accessories

*F*or the next two days, Isabelle tried to be the best trainee ever. She also tried to stay out of Angelica's way. But this was not easy because the Bests kept putting Angelica and Isabelle together.

So, together, Angelica and Isabelle turned rags into dresses. They turned ripe fruit into all kinds of baubles and decorations (mostly useless, but nice). They even managed to make a flower grow as tall as the room. Isabelle wasn't sure if Angelica was covering for her or if she was getting stronger, but the magic was working, so at least for those two days, she didn't complain.

The fourth morning of training, Zahara told everyone to join her in a circle. She waved her wand and a big box appeared on Grandmomma's desk.

"I'd like each of you to choose one item," Zahara instructed the trainees. "Then we'll make some magic."

Angelica asked, "Does that mean team challenges are over?" When Zahara nodded, everyone looked relieved. Angelica pumped her fist. Then she reached into the box and pulled out a really old and dusty necklace. "This looks a million years old."

Zahara smiled. "It belonged to one of my princesses, a mighty queen named Cleopatra. So it's more like 2,085 years old, give or take a decade."

Minerva grabbed an old shoe with a broken buckle. Fawn chose some matchsticks. Irene took a tarnished oil lamp, and MaryEllen took a tattered piece of cloth. By the time Isabelle had a chance, the only thing left was an old spoon.

Next, Zahara asked them all to hold out their hands so that they could receive a sparkle to place on the tips of their wands. Technically, it was a fourth of a sparkle, and all they were going to get to complete this task.

Isabelle's hand shook. When she tried to put the tiny sparkle on her wand, it fluttered to the ground. Then somewhere between her fingers and her wand, it stuck to her sleeve. A third time, it settled on Minerva's head.

Isabelle carefully plucked the sparkle off a white strand of Minerva's hair. "Sorry," she said nervously. But finally, she was ready to go.

Zahara swished her wand like a conductor. "For a moment, I want you to think about your first practice princess. Did she have mementos? Things that you could turn into magical accessories?"

Thinking about Nora's memory box made Isabelle think about the missing sparkles. It also made her think about lost mothers, particularly her own. She wondered why she didn't have anything to remember her mother by. Did Clotilda have something? Was Grandmomma keeping it hidden? Why hadn't Isabelle ever asked? She hoped Grandmomma didn't think she didn't miss Mom.

Then Isabelle heard Zahara say her name, along with the instructions to *pay attention, please.* "Use these memories to help you figure out what might have made your last assignment easier," Zahara said.

This was confusing. So the Bests demonstrated what she meant.

Raine pointed her wand at a teacup. Pop! Pop! Pop! "My cup offers wisdom to anyone who drinks from it."

Kaminari aimed her wand at an old key. Pop! Pop! Pop! "This key will not open a door that endangers a princess."

Clotilda was about to demonstrate, but Minerva told her not to waste the sparkle. She was ready to go. Faster than Minerva had ever moved before, she stepped up and pointed her wand at the old shoe. Right away: Pop! Pop!

Pop! Pop! And then . . . hiss! The buckle on the strap turned orange, and the shoe itself looked new.

Minerva stood up straighter than usual. She said, "This shoe finds friends." That was a twist. Throughout fairy godmother history, shoes usually led to love.

"What happens if the person isn't a friend?" Isabelle asked without raising her hand. She had to know!

"Why, they get blisters, of course," Minerva said, winking. She handed the shoe to Isabelle. "Should we try it?"

Zahara didn't think that was a good use of time. She grabbed the shoe and handed it back to Minerva. "Fawn, why don't you go next?"

"Okay," Fawn said, pointing her wand at the book of matchsticks. At first, nothing happened. No pop. No hiss. Not even a *pffft*. But then Fawn straightened her elbow and her wand turned bright pink. Two pops and a tiny puff of snow-white dust came out of her wand.

Fawn smiled at Kaminari. She shook out her hand. "That made my fingers tingle."

Zahara picked up the matchsticks. "And they're still hot," she said as she handed them to Fawn. "Nice job. What do they do?"

Fawn looked very excited and proud. "The matchsticks light the way when a princess is lost."

Isabelle raised her hand. She wanted to try them out. She wondered if the matchsticks worked for long journeys or just short ones. But Zahara thought she was volunteering.

"Go ahead, Isabelle," Zahara said. "Since you're so anxious, let's see what you can do."

Isabelle put her spoon on the table in front of her and raised her wand. She straightened her elbow and pointed her wand and thought about Nora. She didn't know how a spoon could've made things easier. But she did remember how her stepmom made all sorts of good foods to make Nora happy. And then a teeny, tiny puff of chocolate-colored dust appeared.

"This spoon will make everything taste yummy," Isabelle announced.

When no one looked impressed, Zahara magically filled a bowl with something that looked a little like broccoli, a little like Brussels sprouts, and smelled a lot like it had been sitting around for a few days.

"Let's test it," Zahara said. When Luciana looked annoyed (she hadn't tested the others), Zahara added, "I'm hungry!" Then she handed the spoon to Angelica.

Hesitantly, Angelica took a taste. Then she spat the nibble into a napkin. "Yuck! Did you do that on purpose? That food tastes disgusting. It's way too sour."

Just to make sure Angelica wasn't joking, Zahara dipped the spoon in the bowl and took the tiniest of tastes. "She's right, kid," she said to Isabelle. "But it was a good sentiment. And not for nothing, this would be great at keeping princesses away from evil potions."

Angelica raised her hand. "Can I take my turn?"

She pointed her wand at the ugly necklace, and right away, sprays of sparkly black-and-red dust shot out of her wand, sending everyone (especially Zahara and Minerva) into coughing fits.

"It looks like someone's been practicing," Raine said approvingly.

Angelica didn't deny it. She said, "The jewels on this necklace will turn red if someone·has a secret." Then she slipped it around her neck to test it out.

When Angelica faced Fawn, nothing happened. When she faced the Worsts, the jewels turned pink. But the Worsts were old. Of course they had secrets. They were probably really old secrets, too.

Then Angelica faced Isabelle, and the necklace turned bright red. "I knew it!" Angelica said.

Isabelle didn't want to lie—but confessing was out of the question. She didn't want to get in trouble or get Nora or Grandmomma in trouble—and she was pretty sure that all of them would. Most of all, she didn't want to give Angelica the upper hand. Not today. Not when Grandmomma had just trusted her.

So she took a deep breath and said what is known in the business of fibs as a half truth. "My secret is that I didn't read the rule book. Not any of it. I didn't even open my Wish List until after I met Nora. I was so clueless that Clotilda had to scold me until I studied." Then Isabelle apologized again to Angelica about the rose. And this time, Zahara urged Angelica to accept Isabelle's apology.

"Class dismissed," Luciana said, shooing them out the door. "Practice your wand work. And see you in three days for testing. Clotilda? Can you hold on a second? I need to speak to you."

"And I want to talk to you," Angelica said to Isabelle as they filed out of the training center. Unfortunately, there was no getting away from her.

"What about?" Isabelle asked. She tried not to look nervous. "I already told you my secret. You already embarrassed me."

Angelica narrowed her eyes at Isabelle. "I want to talk to you because my necklace hasn't changed back. So you must be lying. Or there's something else you're not telling us."

Isabelle thought about running. She didn't want to get into a grudge match with Angelica. (There was no way she'd ever win.) She also didn't want to be caught in a lie.

"Well, maybe it's just cooling off," Isabelle said, trying her best to look nonchalant. "Or maybe your magic isn't perfect."

Angelica gave Isabelle a look that said she was pretty confident her magic was the best. If not perfect, nearly.

"Then why has everyone been acting so strangely?" Angelica asked, scowling in an unhappily-ever-after way. "Why do you think they keep putting us together? All the Bests know the only reason you're still here is because of your grandmother. They all believe you're going to end up in the Home. Or even worse. Just like *her*."

Isabelle was sure that if the Bests really felt that way, Clotilda would tell her. But maybe Clotilda had. Maybe that's why she gave her that cheat sheet. "I'm sorry you think I'm lying. And that I'm not very good at magic." Isabelle just wanted to go home. "But leave my mom out of it. She wasn't really that bad, she was just misunderstood."

Angelica laughed in a not-nice way. "Misunderstood? The way I heard it, your mother was the most careless, irresponsible, worst fairy godmother ever. If it wasn't for her, all of us would be much happier."

Isabelle knew that gossip in the fairy godmother world could get out of hand. She knew the truth. But still, she couldn't help herself. "What did they tell you?"

Chapter Nine

The Very Short and Sad Story of the Most Unhappy Princess, According to Angelica

Warning: This is a very sad story. It is the story of a very unhappy princess and her fairy godmother, Isabelle's mother. No matter how much we want it to end differently, it will always end the same way—unhappily ever after. (If you want to see Clotilda's version, see *The Wish List #1: The Story of the Worst Fairy Godmother, According to Clotilda*.)

Once upon a time, a long time ago, before the fairy godmothers wised up and made themselves a rule book and a training program, there was a very simple princess who wanted simple things and a simple life. She had all the qualities that princesses desired: beauty, wisdom, and the admiration of the world. Even better, the sweetest, simplest prince in the world had already fallen in love with her.

Happily ever after seemed like a slam dunk.

That's why the very powerful and bossy fairy godmother in charge of assignments deployed her daughter, a very new fairy godmother, to help the simple princess. You see, the fairy godmother had ambitions for her daughter. She convinced her friends that her daughter could do the job better than anyone else.

At the time, it didn't seem like a big deal. All of the best fairy godmothers were overworked. For this princess, they decided the newbie could get it done.

Unfortunately, they were wrong.

Very wrong.

This fairy godmother was a terrible fairy godmother. She didn't teach her princess to be independent. She didn't listen to her princess's wishes. She didn't heed the warnings that sparkles should be used in moderation. She failed so many times, her princess begged her to leave or to give her a new fairy godmother, but she wouldn't.

The beautiful princess was so miserable she stopped being a princess. She gave away her crown and everything she loved, and settled into a life of complete and utter despair.

The rest of the story everyone knows.

Because everyone loved the simple princess so much, they stopped believing in magic. They stopped trusting their fairy godmothers. They stopped believing in happily ever after. And there is no ending worse than that.

In Clotilda's version, Mom had been a selfless fairy god-mother. She loved her princess so much she granted every single wish and more! The problem had been the princess. She had wanted too much.

But in this version, Isabelle's mom sounded careless and self-centered. Grandmomma seemed short-sighted.

Angelica said, "I don't know why we just can't say it. Your family is to blame for everything—and don't think we don't know it. No offense, but I don't know why they even let you in this class. Everyone knows you're just like her. I'm sorry, but someone needs to tell you. No one, not even Minerva, thinks you can do it."

For a moment, Isabelle stood there. She respected Angelica's magic. She was a great trainee. Unlike Isabelle, Angelica practiced. She read the books. She didn't need every sparkle.

Isabelle knew she hadn't earned Angelica's respect, but she thought Minerva was her friend.

She was determined not to cry. Or throw up. (Even though she wanted to do both.)

Instead, Isabelle said, "I'm going to do everything possible to prove you wrong." Then she took off for home and tried not to worry about Mom or Grandmomma or even the upcoming test. But that was hard. Angelica's version of the story hurt. It made Isabelle question everything.

Isabelle wanted to stand up for Mom. But this was the problem with gossip. Isabelle couldn't stop wondering which story was true.

Maybe Mom was the problem.

Maybe Isabelle was the problem, too.

For the first time since she started training, Isabelle wondered if maybe it wasn't the rules that were wrong. Maybe it was her. Maybe Angelica was right. Maybe she should just give up.

Chapter Ten

A Princess Twist

After three days of sitting with the girlgoyles, talking to Clotilda, and snacking on everything she could get her hands on, Isabelle no longer believed everything Angelica had told her. But she wasn't totally confident, either.

It didn't help that when she arrived at the center (with her book and her pencil), everyone else was already there. Luciana stood at the front of the classroom. Raine, Kaminari, Clotilda, and Zahara were there, too. All of them looked very solemn, as though they had terrible news.

"What's wrong?" Isabelle asked, taking her seat. "Did something happen to Grandmomma?"

Zahara patted Isabelle on the head.

"Of course not," she whispered. "They're just being dramatic. You'll see."

Luciana tapped her wand on her desk. "We actually have good news. It has been our honor to prepare you for this next, important step. All of you have worked hard. You have proven that you have fortitude and grit. So after careful deliberation and debate, we have decided not to formally test you. All of you deserve the chance to help a new practice princess."

When Isabelle heard "no testing," she forgot everything Angelica had said about her and Mom and how she didn't belong. Instead, she jumped out of her seat and twirled in the aisle and shared high fives with Minerva, Irene, and MaryEllen. She almost gave Clotilda a hug, but Clotilda told her to settle down and keep calm.

Only Fawn and Angelica looked a little bit unhappy. "You mean we studied for nothing?"

Kaminari gave them each a sour drop and a big yellow chrysanthemum. "I know it's a disappointment, but trust me, you'll be better godmothers for it."

When she was done consoling them, Luciana asked Raine to hand out the sealed envelopes.

"Inside your packet, you will find your Level Two practice princess as well as a small parcel of carefully measured sparkles to load into your wands," Luciana announced.

Zahara reminded them of other things they knew: that they'd have one season (or six weeks) to make their practice princesses happily ever after. And that they wouldn't get any more sparkles, even if they needed them, because of the circumstances.

Isabelle couldn't help but notice that Zahara had not mentioned regular girls. She wondered if this meant she was getting a practice princess. But maybe Zahara had just forgotten that regular girls could now get fairy godmothers.

Angelica and Fawn opened theirs first. They didn't smile like they had during Level One training (but maybe they were still miffed about the test). Minerva opened hers next, and she seemed downright angry. She stood up, walked down the aisle, and handed the envelope to Zahara. "I'm sorry, but this must be a mistake."

Zahara handed the envelope back. She told Minerva it was not a mistake. In fact, it was a perfect assignment. She called it an extra special challenge for her fortitude.

Minerva would not back down. "Perhaps you don't understand what an uncomfortable position you are putting me in."

But apparently, Zahara did understand. Perfectly.

For a tiny old fairy godmother, Zahara could look pretty scary, especially when she was annoyed. She told Minerva, "You knew you shouldn't have gotten so attached to your first practice princess. Perhaps you're not as loyal to the job as you say you are."

Minerva reminded Zahara that her Level One practice princess had been the great-great-great-granddaughter of her first beloved princess—and that it was way too late to tell her not to get attached. She had cared for the family for years. At the last Extravaganza, she'd requested to make the young princess happily ever after when she graduated from Level Four.

But Zahara didn't care. "Either make this new practice princess happily ever after or . . . do I have to remind you of Rule Four B?"

Now Minerva sat down. "No, you don't have to remind me."

But Isabelle had no clue what that rule was for. "I thought Three C was the bad one."

Fawn shook her head. "Isabelle, Rule Four B says that if you don't do what you're supposed to do, you're finished. Back to Level One."

At the word *finished*, the Worsts huddled around Minerva.

Luciana tapped her wand until the Worsts sat down and stopped talking. "Trainees, please settle down. We have no intention of returning any of you to Level One. Or making *any* of your practice princesses unhappy." When no one would settle down, she tapped her wand on her desk. "But we are serious about these assignments. They will test your loyalty. And your focus." Now she raised her wand in the air. "So keep calm. Trust the sparkles. Open up your envelopes and check your Wish Lists! I understand that some of your princesses have already made wishes!"

Isabelle opened her envelope. She hoped for a practice princess who had already wished. (That meant not so much waiting!)

The first thing she found was a teeny tiny packet of raw sparkles—it was less than a teaspoon—less than she'd needed to make Nora happily ever after.

But that wasn't a surprise. Isabelle was getting used to rationing.

So she took a look at the enclosed photo.

She was another regular girl, not a practice princess. She had very long blond hair that she kept up in a high ponytail. Like Nora, she hadn't wished yet. Unlike Nora, at least she was smiling. Her T-shirt was cute. It said AIM FOR THE STARS.

She looked nice. Isabelle wasn't sure why Minerva had been so upset.

"Do you recognize her?" Clotilda asked.

The truth was, Isabelle didn't. So she looked again. She thought back to everything she had done with Nora, and then Isabelle figured it out.

The girl in the photo was one of the girls Isabelle had met with Nora in the park—one of the girls Nora no longer talked to. Isabelle didn't know more than that because Nora had been too hurt to explain what had gone wrong.

Isabelle remembered how mad and uncomfortable and sad Nora was when Isabelle suggested that the girl might be nice.

Her name was Samantha T. Butterfield.

Isabelle had a feeling the *T* stood for *trouble*. Whatever Samantha wanted, Isabelle had a feeling it was going to involve Nora.

Chapter Eleven

Clotilda in Charge

All the way home, Isabelle and Clotilda argued. It wasn't the first time. They *were* sisters. When something terrible happened, this was what they did.

"I told you to be ready for anything," Clotilda reminded her in that older perfect sister know-it-all way.

Isabelle said, "But why did they have to give me an ex-friend of Nora's? Isn't that sort of mean?" Fairy godmothers, she was 99.9 percent sure, were always supposed to be nice. Never mean. She asked, "Isn't there a big chance that Samantha will want something that will make Nora unhappy?"

When they got home and there was no truce (or answers) in sight, Clotilda went to her room and Isabelle said good-bye and gladly went to hers.

In her room, Isabelle made a plan. First, she waited as quietly as she could until she was positive Clotilda had gone to bed. Then she tiptoed down the hall, past Clotilda's closed door, to Grandmomma's office and the Official Fairy Godmother Spyglass. There was no better, faster way to see what Samantha was up to.

When she got to Grandmomma's office, she pulled hard on the big brass handle, opened the gigantic door, and found her sister sitting behind Grandmomma's desk.

"I knew it!" Clotilda said. "You were going to cheat."

There was no point in denying it. "Not cheat. Study." Isabelle tried to justify her actions. "Grandmomma let me do it. There's no rule against it."

Clotilda wasn't buying any of Isabelle's excuses. "Well,

Grandmomma put me in charge, and I say no spyglass or anything else out of the ordinary. Got it?"

Clotilda ushered Isabelle back into the hall and locked the office door behind them.

"Isabelle, if you are going to be a great fairy god-mother, you have to do this the right way. I know the assignments seem sketchy, but it won't be that hard on Nora. I promise."

Isabelle wasn't sure she believed her. She remembered how sad Nora had been when they saw Samantha. She pleaded with her sister. "Are you sure I can't peek? Just once? In the name of happily ever after?"

Clotilda sighed. (She could be a softie when it came to happily ever after.) "Do everything by the book for four-teen days. If you get nowhere, we'll talk."

Fourteen days was a long time.

But it was a compromise.

So Isabelle went back to her room, and for ten days (or nine days more than she wanted to), she did everything

Clotilda told her to do. She loaded the sparkles into her wand, *just in case*. And she waited. And waited. And waited just in case Samantha made her wish. But *just in case* never came.

So, on the eleventh day, she tried sitting between the girlgoyles and continued to wait there. While she waited, she pretended the girlgoyles were Samantha and Nora. She pretended to make them pretty dresses and colorful sneakers. She pretended to make them magic matchsticks and spoons and lie detector necklaces even though girlgoyles obviously never lied.

Pretending to grant wishes is not dawdling. It's also not as much fun as actually granting wishes. And it doesn't make listening for a practice princess (or a regular girl) to wish easier.

But it does make you hungry.

So on the twelfth day, Isabelle headed to the kitchen to bake a cake. Because she was more a cake fan than an icing fan, she made the icing layers very, very thin. When the whole thing was finished, she brought three slices to the girlgoyles and ate them all, because obviously, this was a ploy. Girlgoyles don't eat.

While she ate, she decided to open up the rule book. She glossed over the pictures of fairy godmothers. She wiped some icing off the picture of Clotilda. Then she scanned the index to find out how to make a princess wish faster. But there wasn't a rule about that.

Isabelle did find a rule about determination and enthusiasm and gusto and why those things were good, though. And she also found one about why fairy godmothers don't grant every wish of every girl. Finally, she found the section that explained humility and grace and why fairy godmothers must listen before they grant a wish. She even found a footnote about the number of sparkles and training. She was going to read that (as well as the part about sparkle conservation) but then she stumbled on some pages printed in red letters.

This was Rule Four. It was about probation and other problems.

Rule Four A: A fairy godmother might need to go to retraining, probation, or reassignment to the Fairy Godmother Home for Normal Girls if she

- uses her wands unsafely

- refuses or fails to grant a wish

- is guilty of wasting sparkles

Rule Four B: Fairy godmothers in retraining (also known as Worsts) are automatically on probation. If they fail or refuse to grant a wish (or use too many sparkles) or do anything unsafe, they will need to return to Level One or retire.

Rules Four A and Four B were even worse than Three C. It was so unfair and confusing.

All Isabelle wanted was to make princesses and regular girls happy. She didn't want to be a Best. She just wanted to be good. Or even average. Isabelle threw the book on the ground right between the girlgoyles. The gusts of wind turned the pages one after another until Isabelle spied a page covered in hearts and flowers and mushy testimonials from fairy godmothers. And also princesses. Most of them started, "When I wished on a star . . ."

This gave Isabelle a great idea.

The next morning (or, if you're counting, Day Thirteen), right as the sun began to rise (but Isabelle could still see the moon), she took one sparkle out of her wand and for some reason—she had no idea why—imagined playing catch with her mom. She also imagined Nora's house and then Nora's school and the tree where Isabelle had met Samantha. Maybe Samantha just needed a signal from Isabelle—a reason to wish.

Isabelle used her wand like a magical fishing pole and catapulted the sparkle high into the air. When it hit the sky, it looked like a shooting star.

And then Isabelle listened.

This time, she didn't have to wait long to hear something wonderful. It was singing. A beautiful singing voice. Definitely princess caliber. And whoever she was, she was singing about wishes and all kinds of gifts from the heart.

Isabelle beamed. Clotilda was right! Samantha must be the perfect regular girl for her. She was sure that somewhere in that book it said that fairy godmothers who heard their princess's (or regular girl's) wishes loud and clear had a strong bond and could always grant their wishes, *lickety-split*!

In other words, as Samantha wished, "I really want to be in the show. It doesn't have to be a big part. Just a little one. I really, really, really want it," Isabelle felt a bolt of confidence.

She didn't care that technically, three *really*s did not equal one *I wish*. Isabelle was tired of waiting. She figured an *I want* with some *really*s was as good as an *I wish*. Unfortunately, Isabelle was wrong. But she didn't know that. So she grabbed her packet of sparkles and loaded them into her wand. Then she imagined the tree and puffed down to the regular world.

She landed (with a thump) next to the spot where the *really reallys* had been uttered.

Luckily, it was a quiet thump. And the tree was by some shrubs, so no one saw her. This was a good thing, because one of the difficult parts of getting a regular girl was that regular girls scared easily. They didn't necessarily believe in fairy godmothers. Or at least, Nora hadn't appreciated her arrival. She thought fairy tales and fairy godmothers were all made up.

Down on the ground, Samantha's voice rang in Isabelle's ears. It made her heart swell. Isabelle felt really confident. As she tiptoed around the tree, she was sure she could grant this wish in record time.

At the base of a tree sat a girl. She had unruly hair and a scab on her knee. She was reading a book.

This was not Samantha. The girl who wanted the part (a lot) was Nora.

Chapter Twelve

The Terrifying Discovery

It's nerve-racking when someone sneaks up on you literally out of thin air. It's equally nerve-racking to discover that the wish you just heard was made not by your current practice princess (or regular girl) but by your former practice princess (or regular girl), who also doesn't remember you at all because of (stupid) Rule Three C.

In other words, Isabelle and Nora both jumped and gasped. They both needed a moment to compose themselves.

Nora was the first to stop screaming. "Why did you sneak up on me like that? Did someone ask you to find out what I was doing?"

Isabelle tried not to laugh. She was so happy to see Nora, but the notion was ridiculous.

"No one told me to spy on you," Isabelle said, frantically patting all of her pockets to make sure she hadn't dropped her loaded wand. "I was just taking a walk and looking around. This seemed like a good place to sit down."

"It is a good spot," Nora said, giving Isabelle the stink eye. "Especially if you want to be alone." (In other words, she was not inviting Isabelle to stay.)

Isabelle sat down anyway. It was sort of charming watching Nora be so completely unfriendly. And secretive, too, especially when anyone (even a fairy godmother in training) could see that something important was happening in the schoolyard. In every direction, kids were sitting in circles. Or practicing scenes. Others practiced a cool-looking dance.

"What's going on?" Isabelle said.

"It's the last recess before vacation," Nora replied, looking up from her pages. "Did you just move here? They're practicing for the play. Auditions are tomorrow."

What perfect timing! This meant Isabelle didn't have to go to school. "So why aren't you practicing with them?"

Nora said, "Because I don't think practicing in public is the only way to get ready."

This was what is known as a silly excuse. Nora should have been practicing with everyone else, and she knew it. She just didn't want to admit it.

Isabelle felt bad. She knew this meant that Nora was worried. But she also needed to get things moving along. In other words, she needed to meet Samantha. She asked Nora if it was too late to sign up for the play.

Reluctantly, Nora told Isabelle:

- The play was an annual event.

- It was not too late to sign up.

- It took place during school vacation, and kids from other schools tried out, too.

- She really wanted one specific part. But she probably wouldn't get it. Because of last year.

"What happened last year?" Isabelle asked.

"It's more like what didn't happen." Nora picked at her nails like she was recalling a very bad memory. "First I forgot my line. Then I messed up the dance." She looked over at the kids who were practicing, especially the tall girl in the middle. (It was Samantha!)

Isabelle was torn. And a little guilty. Even though she was here for Samantha, she could see that Nora still needed a friend.

More than ever, she hated Rule Three C.

She held out her hand. (She couldn't help it.) "My name's Isabelle. Pleased to meet you."

"And I'm Nora." Nora asked Isabelle what she liked to do for fun. When Isabelle said "hiking in the woods and making cookies," it seemed that Nora was about to tell her all about cleaning up the world and ending hunger and all the things that Isabelle knew were really important to her. But then the bell rang and the dancing broke up, and two girls and a boy started walking toward Isabelle and Nora. The trio wore matching scarves and gloves. They looked like they couldn't stop dancing.

First they took a big step with the left foot. Then they did the same thing with the right foot. Finally they all stopped, clapped their hands, and did a little twirl.

"They always walk like that," Nora said, getting up to leave. But she wasn't fast enough.

"Hi, Nora," Samantha said. "Who's your friend?" Isabelle didn't know whether to laugh or cry. This was almost exactly what Samantha had asked the last time they all stood here, except, of course, only Isabelle remembered that. When Nora introduced Isabelle, Samantha introduced her friends, Janet and Mason.

"Are you interested in the play, too?" Samantha asked. "Because we can teach you all the moves. But first, we're starved. Want to go to Dairy Twirl for an ice cream sandwich made with chocolate babka?"

It was hard to imagine anything better than an ice cream sandwich made with chocolate babka. Isabelle turned to Nora. "Do you want to go, too?" She crossed her fingers. Maybe Nora would say yes.

"I have other things to do," Nora said, holding up an empty bag that Isabelle knew would soon be filled with garbage she picked up around the schoolyard. Saving the earth was the most important thing to Nora. "But you can go ahead, if you want to."

Isabelle wanted to clean up the world with Nora, but today, she really didn't have a choice.

"Then I guess I'll see you later," Isabelle said. "Good luck with your lines."

Ten to one, Samantha's wish had to do with the play.

Ten to one, Samantha and Nora wanted the same thing.

Chapter Thirteen

Triple Threats Only!

The first thing Samantha, Mason, and Janet did was teach Isabelle "the walk."

"The basic moves are like this," Samantha said. She told Isabelle to watch carefully. "First step forward and to the left. Then forward and to the right. Then kick with your left and shuffle with your right."

It took Isabelle about three tries to get it right. But once she did, she had to admit it was fun to link arms and strut down the street this way. It was also fun adding new moves, like a small jump and a shimmy. (Although Mason refused to do that part.)

As they walked, Samantha told Isabelle more about the play. "After auditions, they hold practices. Then right before the new year, we perform on the big stage at school. And everyone comes and we have a party and flowers, and sometimes they put our pictures in the newspaper."

Isabelle asked, "What if you don't want to be in the play?"

Samantha didn't completely understand not wanting to be on the stage in front of tons of people, but Janet did.

"I always make star-shaped cookies with sparkles and chocolate glaze to sell at intermission." Janet smiled at Samantha. "They're Samantha's favorite. Plus, we give the proceeds to charity. So everyone thinks it's great."

It sounded like fairy godmothers had helped this play before. And that Nora and Janet could be good friends.

"Maybe I'll make something," Isabelle said. Then she started to describe her favorite treats, but Samantha wanted to practice a dance. And a few important lines.

"Samantha should totally get the part of the good witch." Janet then explained that every kid got a part, but Samantha didn't think that was true anymore.

"My dads say that this year they're only taking triple threats," Samantha explained. (In other words, people who were good at dancing, singing, and acting.) "The principal hired this big-time famous writer named Dee to write the play and the songs and even direct. We might even be on TV. Dee's fans are already asking about tickets! So she and the principal are going to be super choosy this year. And we're going to practice a ton more. They don't want anyone to wreck it."

This didn't sound fair. Or fun. It made Isabelle worry that Samantha wasn't always nice. And that Nora was never going to get a part. Even though she now knew Nora had a great voice, she was also pretty sure Nora was not a triple threat. The truth was, Nora would need a little magic to be as good as Samantha.

But Isabelle couldn't think about Nora now. She had to focus on Samantha. And granting her wish. (Not Nora's.)

"So let me get this straight," Isabelle said. "The play's about a good witch? And she makes a lot of magic?"

Samantha nodded. "The play begins when one by one, a bunch of kids—none of them connected—stumble on a well in the middle of a beautiful wood. It turns out to be a magic wishing well that belongs to a horrible witch."

Regular people were so funny. Wells were never magic. They never granted wishes, good or bad. But Isabelle couldn't say this.

She asked, "And the bad witch makes them all miserable?"

"Not exactly," Samantha said, whipping out the script. "The bad witch makes the bad kids unhappy. Then the good witch steps in. She turns those kids around. And in the end, the wishes and the kids turn out great. Good conquers evil! Everyone lives happily ever after!"

Janet said, "Samantha's song is the highlight of the show."

Samantha crossed her fingers. "If I get it."

"Don't be silly," Janet said. "You have to get it!"

Samantha sang a few sappy lines about the power of wishes and good deeds. (It was the same one Isabelle had heard Nora singing.) "She also does a dance with the bad witch and the bad witch's assistant. And at the end, everyone thanks her for being so good."

Mason said, "I'm trying out to be the assistant." He explained that this was mostly because there was no risk of this character having to kiss anyone.

Isabelle was going to ask more, but in front of her was the biggest, brightest, most beautiful place she had ever seen.

It looked like a castle, except the towers were ice cream cones. The steps and the counters were decorated to look just like silver candy wrappers. The windows and door looked like they were made of chocolate and rainbow-striped mints.

Inside was even better. There were over two hundred flavors of ice cream. And you could mix up the flavors with any kind of candy or you could dip your ice cream in chocolate that turned into a shell.

Samantha walked up to the counter and (without asking) ordered, "Four babka sandwiches with quadruple chocolate ice cream dipped in dark chocolate, please." She handed the first one to Isabelle. "Quadruple chocolate might sound simple, but you will never eat anything better than this."

Samantha was not wrong. It was the best ice cream ever—both sweet and a little salty. Like happily ever after or a wish come true.

When they were stuffed to the brim, Janet and Mason picked up their bags to walk home.

This was Isabelle's chance.

"I have something really important to tell you," she told Samantha. But then she burped (very loudly). And Samantha burst into laughter.

This was not the way Isabelle had wanted this to go.

Even worse, Mason came back inside. "My mom's here. You guys want a ride?"

"I never turn down a ride," Samantha said, wiping all the chocolate off her lips. "What about you?"

Obviously, Isabelle didn't need or want a ride. "I'll walk," she said. "But can I come over tomorrow?" She burped again. "To learn the dance? Just in case? And to tell you something important?"

"Sure, why not," Samantha said, writing down her address and handing Isabelle some papers. "Here is the script. I already know the whole thing by heart."

When Isabelle arrived at the castle, she went directly to the girlgoyles and made a plan.

Isabelle would make Samantha happily ever after—it couldn't be that hard. And while she was doing that, she would also bring Samantha and Nora together. Because of the play, that had to be possible. It wouldn't help Nora get the part she wanted, but better than that, Nora would have a friend. And once Samantha and Nora were friends, they could all go to Nora's house, and while they were singing all the best songs from the play, Isabelle could sneak into Nora's room and get back her sparkles. Once they'd been returned, Isabelle was sure that everything would return to normal. No more sparkle shenanigans! And then Grandmomma could come back for Level Three and Isabelle would be a hero. (Or at least, not in trouble.)

It wasn't easy peasy, lemon squeezy, but it was a plan. Hopefully it was doable.

For her sake, Nora's sake, and the sake of the fairy godmother world (if she was being dramatic), Isabelle would have to try.

Chapter Fourteen

I Am Your Fairy Godmother

The next morning, Isabelle got up early. She brushed her hair and put it in a high ponytail. She put on her nicest jeans and sparkly green sneakers.

In other words, she tried to look like a regular girl. With a little extra pizzazz.

When she showed up at Samantha's door, she was relieved to find that Janet and Mason weren't there.

"I have something important to tell you before we go to the audition," Isabelle said right away.

But Samantha also had something important to show Isabelle. (And if it wasn't yet clear, Samantha always got her way.)

"What do you think?" Samantha asked, twirling in a circle.

"About what?"

"About my dress! Isn't it beautiful? Aren't the wings cool? I know it's a fairy godmother costume, but it was all I had. Besides, aren't good witches and fairy godmothers basically the same thing?"

Her dress was beautiful—almost as sparkly and pink as Clotilda's last Extravaganza dress—but those wings had to go.

Fairy godmothers and good witches (whatever they were) were not the same thing. Even worse, fairy godmothers only had wings in books, not in real life. "So, about that important thing I wanted to tell you . . ."

Samantha didn't hear her. Instead, she introduced Isabelle to the fattest, fluffiest cat Isabelle had ever seen,

Prince Oberon the Fifth. Samantha told Isabelle to keep a distance. "Unless he moves his tail. That means he wants to be picked up."

They stared at his tail for five minutes. But that tail didn't move, not even a smidge. So they left him alone.

Instead, Samantha demonstrated her dance moves. And her big song. And part of the song she would sing with the bad witch (which was an even better song, but not a solo).

She would have kept practicing and singing and dancing and flapping those dumb wings, but Isabelle shouted, "Samantha, please stop! For just for a second. I need to tell you something important. Fairy godmothers don't have wings. In fact, wings arc sort of disrespectful."

Samantha laughed. "What are you talking about?"

"It's what I've been trying to tell you." Isabelle whipped out her wand and tried to stand as tall as possible. "I am your fairy godmother. I am here to make you happily ever after."

Samantha laughed so hard Prince Oberon swished his tail. "You are hilarious," she said, picking up the cat and scratching his head. "Can we pull this on Mason? He's always complaining that boys never get wishes."

"No, we cannot do that," Isabelle replied. Instead of explaining the rules (and wasting precious time), she pointed her wand at a fuzzy gray yarn ball in the corner of the room. It was Prince Oberon's toy mouse. "You need proof?" Isabelle took a deep breath and imagined the yarn running through a field. Or across the kitchen floor.

For a moment, nothing happened.

But Isabelle did not give up. She straightened her elbow and thought about determination. Then she envisioned Samantha and Nora on the stage. And to her surprise, it happened. Pop! Pop! Pop! Hiss! The yarn turned into an extremely frightened mouse! Luckily, Samantha was still holding Prince Oberon. By the time he wiggled free, the mouse had run out the open door to the woods outside.

Samantha did a little victory dance (unlike Nora, who had called for the police). Like Nora, she asked a ton of questions. "How does anyone choose? Can we tell Janet? Can I ask my dads?" Samantha paced in a circle. "This doesn't have to be about love, does it? This is real life, you know. Not a fairy tale."

Isabelle agreed. "No, it definitely doesn't have to have anything to do with love. All you have to do is make a wish that you know in your heart will make you . . ."

"Happily ever after!" Samantha rubbed her hands together. "Oh, this is going to be so perfect." Then she sat down. "How long do I have to decide?"

Isabelle counted all the days on her fingers. "By my calculation, you have exactly four weeks. But you can wish now. If you know what you want." She winked. "Like a perfect audition, perhaps?"

To Isabelle's surprise, Samantha didn't jump all over that. "I don't know. Maybe I should become a real princess with a real live kingdom and a gigantic castle. Or can I wish to be famous? On TV or on the stage? Can you make me the youngest president ever? Can you help me invent something that will change the entire world? Or can I wish for more wishes?"

Again the wish for more wishes. Regular girls were so unreasonable.

Isabelle begged Samantha to come up with something smaller (in other words, doable). "Why don't you want to wish to get the part of the good witch?"

Samantha told her that would not be necessary.

"Are you sure?" Isabelle asked.

"One hundred percent," Samantha replied. "Officially, I have to act like I might not get the part, but the truth is, no one else has a chance, and not just because I've been the star of every play since I was old enough to read. My dads know Dee. They told me the part is mine."

Isabelle sat down. This was a big disappointment. And not fair at all. "So there's nothing I can do right now?"

"Of course there is," Samantha said. "Stick around. Cheer me on. Come to the audition. I'll even take off the wings." She told Isabelle to put her wand away. "When I know what I want, you'll be the first to hear about it."

So that's what they did.

Isabelle went to the audition with Samantha, Mason, and Janet. (Even though Janet wasn't auditioning, she stuck to Samantha like glue.)

Samantha was, indeed, a triple threat. Her song was great. Her dancing was perfection. She didn't mess up a single line.

Mason was pretty good, too. Dee asked him to do a lot of funny things, like crawl on the ground and swing from a imaginary vine and pretend to have a New York accent. Isabelle didn't know why this was important, but she could see that Dee thought it was great.

While Dee tried teaming him up with a girl named Teja—to turn the witch's assistant into a two-headed assistant—Isabelle looked for Nora. She was sitting in the corner. Her hair was wilder than ever. And she looked terrified.

Isabelle felt bad. "When are you up?" she asked.

"Right after Mason and Teja," Nora said. "I practiced all day. I think I'm ready."

"What part do you want?"

She smiled. "The good witch. But since I'll never get it, I decided to go for the bad one." She picked up her fake wand and pointed it at Isabelle. "Do I look scary? I don't, right?" She put the fake wand down. "I don't know what I'm even doing here." She got up and walked to the back of the room to pace.

Isabelle picked up Nora's fake wand. It was sort of sad. It looked like a plain black stick.

Even though she was sure this was totally against the rules, Isabelle had to do something for Nora. She tapped the tip of her wand and secretly removed a teeny tiny fleck of sparkle—just enough for one night's worth of happiness. As Isabelle pressed the sparkle into Nora's fake wand, she imagined Nora having a great audition. And making up with Samantha. And making the whole world cleaner and better. (It was impossible not to cheer for Nora.)

When the fake wand glowed and hissed and sputtered, Isabelle practically jumped out of her seat. But right away, it looked normal—and fake—again. So nobody could tell it held a tiny bit of magic.

When Nora returned, Isabelle gave the fake wand back to her and wished her good luck. For a split second, it looked like maybe Nora remembered something, like she knew who Isabelle was. But then she didn't. She just looked really, really, really happy.

"Have a good time," Isabelle said. "I hope you're the best bad witch ever."

And of course, she was.

Nora still wasn't a triple threat, but she sang with gusto! She only stumbled once. When she said, "Evil children deserve what they wish for," she actually sounded a little bit like Minerva (especially when she was in a bad mood).

126

When Nora was done, Dee called everyone onstage. "Thank you, everyone, for auditioning for the play. I was very excited by what I saw tonight." After quickly going over the bad news—that there weren't enough parts for everyone—she told them, "All of you were great. It's going to make casting very difficult. But I'll get it done. The cast will be posted tonight. First rehearsal is tomorrow. So get some sleep and get ready to work. Once we get started, you need to be ready for anything and everything."

Chapter Fifteen

The Good Witch and the Bad Witch— in Three Short Acts

Act I

No surprise, Samantha got the part of the good witch, and Nora got the part of the bad one. Mason was half of the bad witch's assistant, and Teja, who turned out to be the school's best soccer player, was the other half. Janet decided to help with props. Samantha introduced Isabelle to Dee. "Is it okay if she watches?" She told her that Isabelle was her "professional audience."

At the first rehearsal, Dee spent most of the day talking about "life on the stage," which was another way of saying she talked for a really long time about how hard she worked on the script and how to get into the mood to act and that she had written many books, but this was her first play, and that she was excited to say something "important" and "meaningful" about the nature of good and evil.

Isabelle couldn't help noticing that Samantha wrote down every word she said.

And so did Nora.

She also noticed that both Samantha and Nora had the same kind of notebook. And the same kind of pen. Isabelle caught them staring at each other when they didn't think the other was looking.

During a break, Isabelle asked Janet what that was about (even though she knew).

Janet explained that Samantha and Nora used to be best friends. But then one day, they weren't.

"I wish they'd both get over themselves and make up," Janet said.

Isabelle wished Janet were her regular girl. She could grant that wish right now. "Do you have any theories?"

Janet talked quietly, so no one else could hear. "All I know is that they're both miserable! And so am I! I miss doing things with Nora. Neither one of them is ever going to be really happy until they make up."

So the next day, Isabelle decided to see what she could do without sparkles. (Remember: She didn't have that many.) She suggested to Samantha, Janet, Nora, and Mason that they all get together after practice—to practice some more.

Samantha shrugged. "As long as we practice at my house."

Unfortunately, Nora refused. (Mostly because of Prince Oberon. She had bad allergies.) "Why can't we practice at mine?" When Samantha wouldn't budge, Nora suggested that Isabelle come to her house alone. That made Samantha so mad she almost looked like the bad witch instead of the good one.

For the rest of the first week, neither one of them would give in, so Isabelle had no choice but to stick with Samantha. They practiced at school. And then they went home. Or to the Dairy Twirl. It seemed that every chance she got, Samantha complained about Nora.

"She's so serious. And so inflexible. Did you see the way she messed up the dance? She kept standing and singing right in front of me." Samantha crossed her arms over her chest and stamped her foot. "I wish Nora Silverstein had never tried out for the play." Then she covered her mouth. Because of the word *wish*.

Isabelle knew this wasn't official. "Don't worry, I understood what you meant."

Samantha looked relieved. "Knowing Nora, she's messing up on purpose just to get on my nerves."

It was really frustrating. Even though Samantha said she'd never be happy until Nora performed up to speed,

Isabelle was pretty sure Samantha's happily ever after had less to do with the play and more to do with friendship. The problem was, all these practices (and trips back and forth from the fairy godmother world) took a lot of sparkle power. So she just had to hope that Nora's dancing got better. She didn't have enough sparkles to experiment too much.

Act II

By the middle of the second week of practice, Nora was still struggling. She was still standing when she should be sashaying. And tiptoeing when she should be stomping. So Dee called an extra practice for Samantha, Nora, Mason, and Teja.

She made them do it four times. But each time, something went terribly wrong.

First Mason didn't want to hold hands with Teja. Then Nora stepped on Samantha's toe. Then Dee thought "the composition" was wrong and made everyone change places, and then she even added some lines—two for Nora and one for Mason. And then Nora stepped on Samantha's toe again.

"I think it's broken," Samantha complained.

(It wasn't.)

When they finally got through the scene without Dee having to yell "Cut," Dee asked Samantha to "take five" so she could work with just Nora all by herself. After that, she'd work with Samantha. And then maybe they'd do the whole thing one more time.

Samantha did not like this at all. She hated waiting. More than that, she hated going second. She thought that Dee was paying more attention to Nora, and then she began wondering if she should have wished for someone other than Nora to get the part. "I thought this was supposed to be a professional production, but Nora walks around like she has two left feet."

It was the perfect time to use some sparkle power.

(Just a tiny bit.)

Before Nora took the stage, Isabelle put a sparkle fleck on Nora's fake wand. She told herself she was doing this to help Samantha relax, but the truth was, Isabelle also wanted Nora to be great. And with half a sparkle of confidence, she danced pretty well.

When Dee called Samantha to the stage for her dance, Isabelle got another fleck ready. Then she sat down next to Nora.

"I wish my mom could see this," Nora said. Then she told Isabelle all the things she already knew. That her mom had died. And that even though she loved her stepmom, she missed her mom every day.

"What's your family like?" she asked Isabelle. "Are they coming to the play?"

Isabelle told her they were still too busy getting settled in. Because that seemed like not enough of an excuse, she also told Nora that she had a sister and that her sister was making "life difficult."

Nora understood completely. "My brother can be a pain,

too. You know, Dee is letting him introduce the show before they open the curtain. My stepmom thinks it'll be really cute. He practices all day." Nora mimicked him. "Welcome to the *Secret of the Magic Wishing Well.*" She rolled her eyes. When she said *well*, she held it for a really long time.

Isabelle laughed. "You're funny."

Nora smiled. "No, I'm not. At least, that's what Samantha says." She looked at her lines and her ex-friend and got ready to go back onstage. "I wish I could be as good as her. And funny. It would be great to make everyone laugh."

Isabelle knew she shouldn't, but two more sparkles couldn't hurt. "When I don't think I can do something, my grandmomma says that practice makes perfect." She pressed the sparkles directly into Nora's hand and wished her luck. "My sister likes to give me sparkles. She tells me to keep calm and sparkle on."

Nora stared at the glitter in her hand. "Thanks, Isabelle. I love it! My auntie Viv is into glitter, too. She calls it magic dust! I have a feeling you're going to like her."

Act III

For the next week and the one after that (so almost the entire fairy godmother season), Dee made the cast practice every single day, morning, noon, and night, until everyone knew their lines and their steps and their cues. By then, they were all exhausted, and frankly, no one cared about the secret of the well, magic or not.

The experience should have brought Samantha and Nora together, but it didn't. Instead, every time they stepped onstage, they seemed to like each other a little bit less.

On the plus side, with and without a little sparkle magic, at least Nora was improving. With each rehearsal, she seemed a little more confident and a little less nervous. Now, when Dee wanted someone to sing louder, she sometimes meant Samantha. When Dee wanted to review a dance, it was because Samantha forgot a step, not Nora.

Janet blamed Dee. She thought she was putting too much pressure on all of them. "It's a school play. It doesn't have to be perfect."

Samantha disagreed. "Of course it has to be perfect. This is my big opportunity. If I want to be a famous actress, this has to be great."

By the morning of the dress rehearsal, Isabelle was sick of practice. She was sick of waiting. She reminded Samantha she had a deadline. "I think you should wish for a great performance."

Samantha didn't want to "waste" her wish on one event. (She was down, but still confident.) "My problem isn't me. It's Nora. When she messes up, we'll all look silly."

Isabelle didn't think she was being completely honest. "You're not worried about being upstaged, are you?" Even though her wand was starting to feel dangerously light, she plucked a sparkle from her wand. "Are you sure you don't know what you want?" Isabelle asked.

Samantha was only sure that she wasn't sure. "Why don't you go home and come back tomorrow," she said. "I've saved my wish this long. Are you sure I can't wish for a whole bunch of wishes?"

Isabelle knew an emergency when she was in one. She had to do something—something she didn't want to do.

She puffed herself back to the fairy godmother castle as fast as she could.

She had to ask Clotilda for help.

She knocked on her sister's door and got ready to grovel.

Chapter Sixteen

Sparkle Mayhem!

"Took you long enough," Clotilda said.

Isabelle flopped onto her sister's perfectly made bed. "She won't make her wish! I don't know what to do."

As Clotilda paced around the room, Isabelle shook out her wand and counted her sparkles. She was down to eight. (This wasn't a lot.)

Clotilda wasn't really in the mood to hear her sister's complaints. "You gave her a deadline?"

"I did."

"Do you know what she might want?"

"I do, but she won't wish for that. She's too focused on the play."

This was the problem. Even though it seemed that Samantha had everything, she'd never be happy until she was friends with Nora again.

"Have you heard from Grandmomma?" Isabelle asked.

"Just to check in. Nothing big," Clotilda said, walking around her room, not making eye contact.

Clotilda might be the fourth best fairy godmother, but she was a terrible liar.

"You know, I know what Grandmomma's doing," Isabelle said.

"Then you should also know that there's more mayhem going on than ever!"

Now Isabelle was concerned. "What do you mean?" she asked.

Clotilda looked unusually eager to get this off her chest. "Angelica's new princess wished to win the annual regatta that her first princess was sailing." Isabelle was pretty sure this didn't seem like that big a deal for a godmother with Angelica's skills, but apparently she was wrong. Clotilda said, "Just as her first princess was approaching the coast of Greece, the water turned choppy. She couldn't control her sail. Her boat nearly capsized."

Isabelle had to agree that must have been terrifying. "But it didn't capsize. And the right princess won? Everyone got to shore safely?"

"That's not the point." Clotilda stamped her foot and paced around the room. "It was supposed to be a little race between rivals. Instead, it felt like someone or something was making mischief."

Isabelle had never heard Clotilda doubt anything in the fairy godmother world. "What about Fawn?"

"Her new practice princess wanted desperately to ski—for whatever reason—please don't ask me. So Fawn made another snowstorm. That should have been easy peasy, but then just like Angelica's, her wish went rogue!

In this case, the snow kept coming. And coming. And her poor princess skied, but she didn't wish for the whole eastern half of the globe to get snowed in. Luckily, her first practice princess had the determination of ten princesses. She helped dig everyone out. Before she was done, she saved three puppies and a cat and even a goldfish."

Isabelle made a mental note not to do anything that depended on weather. "And Minerva?" she asked.

"Minerva is in the wind." (In other words, Clotilda wasn't sure.) "She used her sparkles to help her first princess." Clotilda shook her head. "Zahara is taking it personally. I doubt either one of them will be at the Extravaganza."

"Why do you think this is happening?" Isabelle asked.

Clotilda shut her door, even though no one else was in the castle to snoop. "Things are so bad that Luciana won't even let me visit Melody. Did you hear about her spill?" She wrung her hands with worry. "Grandmomma and the Bests are convinced that *someone's* up to no good."

A feeling of dread came over Isabelle. "You don't think it's Mom, do you?"

Clotilda paced around her room. "I hope not," she said. "But who knows? Maybe her heart turned dark? Maybe being away for this long changes you."

"Clotilda," Isabelle said, "bad things happen. It can't be her."

Clotilda sighed. "Listen. Whatever you do, be on the lookout for anything or anyone that looks odd. But most of all, make Samantha happily ever after, and do it quickly. Tomorrow's the play, right? Well, let's hope she gets some stage fright and wants to use her wish on something straightforward like that. Or maybe some nice boy will come to watch her. Be ready for anything, and then come back home."

With a warning like that, Isabelle had to go straight to the girlgoyles. (There was no better place to think.) She felt like everything was off-balance, especially her. If Grandmomma thought that Mom was sabotaging wishes, it meant Isabelle's mom had turned bad. But it also meant that she was actually out there in the regular world. Isabelle held up her wand and catapulted one tiny sparkle into the sky. (It was all she could spare.) She hoped that maybe tonight, Nora and Samantha could figure things out. More than that, she hoped that Mom was out there, and that she was looking up at the sky. Maybe she could even see Isabelle's sparkle. And wish her back some luck.

Chapter Seventeen

"Break a Leg" Is Just a Saying

The next day, Isabelle arrived at Samantha's house first thing in the morning. This was a good thing, because just as Clotilda had predicted, Samantha was in a tizzy.

Her hair was too wavy.

Her shoes felt a little tight.

The dress rehearsal had not gone well. Samantha's throat felt a tiny bit scratchy. Not scratchy enough to cancel, but just scratchy enough so that one of her dads was busy making tea with honey and toast with cinnamon and sugar while the other one had gone out to get a babka ice cream sandwich, since that always made Samantha feel better.

Isabelle got out her wand. "So, do you want to wish? Shall I make everything perfect?"

"That's not going to be enough." Samantha paced around the room. "Last night, Nora sounded better than me. It was like she had her own fairy godmother! Dee couldn't get enough of her. All Dee cared about was Nora, Nora, Nora, Nora. She kept calling her an unknown talent. And she couldn't believe how amazing her hair looked. You'd think she never saw teased hair before." Then Samantha looked at Isabelle's hair and apologized. "No offense."

Isabelle shrugged. The truth was, she liked her puffy hair. "Are you sure I can't convince you to wish?"

Samantha shook her head. "Not yet." First, she wanted to get there early. She also wanted to practice her song one last time.

She was nervous. (Isabelle could tell.)

When they saw Janet, she noticed, too. "I think the pressure is getting to Samantha," she told Isabelle, giving her a cookie. "It used to just be a fun play. Now no one even wants my cookies. Instead, they hired a caterer!"

Isabelle took a bite. The cast of the play didn't know what they were missing! She spied Nora saying good-bye to her dad; stepmom; her brother, Gregory; and a lady in a long flowery dress and old-fashioned shoes. Isabelle walked over to say hi (and to give Gregory a cookie for luck).

But when she got closer, she almost turned around and ran. Nora's hair and wand were covered in sparkles. "How did you do that?" Isabelle asked. The sparkles—or what Nora called glitter—looked just like the sparkles Isabelle had left in Nora's memory box. Or, in other words: This was going to be a disaster with a capital D.

Nora pointed to the lady in the flowery dress. (She was too busy flicking her wand to notice that Isabelle was freaking out.) "My favorite auntie, Viv, did it." In this case, *favorite* had to be another word for *eccentric*. Or maybe *magical*. Because besides the dress, Viv wore eighteen bracelets on one wrist as well as a ring that looked like it had come out of Zahara's accessory box. And Viv's shoes weren't just old-fashioned. They looked like they were made of gold. But dirty. The way old shoes get when you wear them all the time.

Nora's stepmom said, "When Vivvy and I were little girls, we used to play with glitter all the time. We slept on our braids, too. It's the fastest way to make curly hair magical!"

Isabelle looked at Viv. She didn't know what a rogue fairy godmother looked like. She didn't know if sparkles lost their power if they were exposed to air. Or if her seven sparkles were any match for this.

Viv said, "I could do the same thing with your hair," but Nora said no. She wanted to give the extra glitter to Mason and Teja for their costume, so they could all match. They were already "stuck together" in a special shirt that they shared. They demonstrated their special walk, which wasn't so different from Samantha's.

Once Mason and Teja were covered with sparkles, Nora's family took a whole bunch of pictures of the three of them saying, "We are going to make those kids suffer." Apparently, that was their favorite line from the play, not what they were going to *actually* do. They even asked Samantha to pose for a few photos, but she wouldn't. She was too busy pacing. And worrying. And talking to herself.

This was as bad as a snowstorm. Or a boat capsizing in the sea.

"Meet me in the last stall of the girls' room," Samantha said. Isabelle hoped that meant she was ready to wish.

When Isabelle got there, Samantha was frantic. "I know what I want," she said, pulling Isabelle into the stall and shutting the door. All over the walls were hearts and arrows and drawings and names. In one corner, someone had drawn squares to look like an empty crossword. It looked a little like Isabelle's notebook.

Samantha told Isabelle to focus. "I want Nora to mess up. And I want her to mess up big-time. Can you do that?"

"Are you sure?" Isabelle felt sick to her stomach.

This was not the kind of wish she ever wanted to grant. This wasn't a good wish. This wasn't a nice wish. This couldn't be what Luciana had in mind.

Isabelle also wasn't sure she could do it. All those sparkles on Nora's head—they were not going to wear off quickly. "I could just wish for you to be the best. That would probably work better."

"No," Samantha said. "It's not enough. Make her mess up. Make her fall down. Make her the worst witch ever." She stomped her foot. "And do it now."

Isabelle didn't want to hurt Nora. And this would hurt.

But Isabelle also knew the rules.

Right now, she had to ignore what she was feeling. She had to remember that more than anything, she wanted to be an official fairy godmother. She wanted to be able to come back to the real world again to grant wishes to other regular girls. She really liked the regular world, even with all its silly problems.

As her grandmomma would say, this was the job.

Isabelle whipped out her wand and closed her eyes. She hoped for the best.

She imagined Nora messing up. Falling down. Missing her lines. Then Isabelle flicked her wand with as much enthusiasm as she could, under the circumstances.

Then she turned to Samantha and said, "Your wish is granted."

Samantha didn't even say thank you. (She was too nervous.) Instead, she turned around and stalked out of the bathroom.

The show was about to start.

Chapter Eighteen

Wishing Well and Not So Well

It is not fun waiting for certain disaster to occur onstage.

But Isabelle wouldn't leave. She wanted to be there for Nora and Samantha, too.

The play started with Gregory's announcement. (It went very well.) Then a couple of kids walked onstage and pretended to be spoiled rotten. They made terrible wishes. And then some other kids made some good wishes. And then they all sang songs and did a couple of dances.

In spite of all that practicing, there were some problems.

One little girl had to hold up her tutu to keep it from falling down. And another said her lines to the back of the stage, instead of turning around to face the audience. But when you're little, mistakes are funny. The audience laughs. The people take pictures and they think you're really cute.

That wasn't true when you were older. When you were older, the audience wanted you to be great.

When it was time for Samantha's first big number, Isabelle could barely sit still. Samantha looked just like the best good witch ever, in a big white dress with lots of tulle and ribbons (and thank goodness, no wings). When she hit the high note of the line "Good wishes always get granted," Isabelle clapped her hands with the rest of the audience.

Then it was Nora's turn. Her hair glowed from the sparkles. Her dress twinkled, too—but not in a sweet way. As she marched around the stage, she explained to the audience that the well used to belong to Samantha, but one day, when there was magic in the air, she stole it. She could do that because so many boys and girls made bad wishes.

Then Mason and Teja wobbled onstage to deliver their favorite line, "We are going to make those kids suffer." This was the cue for Nora's big song. Isabelle clutched her wand, even though it was mostly empty.

She wished she could wish. But she couldn't. So she crossed her fingers the way everyone in the regular world does when they want something good to happen.

Nora began her song. "I am the wicked witch of the wishing well," she sang. Then she stepped forward to begin her dance.

She took another step and then two shuffles and then she opened her arms—and BAM! She knocked over the top of the well.

Of course, everybody laughed. (They thought they were supposed to.) Isabelle started to close her eyes, but the funny thing was, Nora didn't look upset. She kept singing.

And smiling. And then she tripped on the top of the well—maybe even on purpose—and that was funny, too. The entire audience was roaring when Mason and Teja wobbled around the stage trying to put it back together. The best part was when Teja went left at the same time Mason went right and with Nora stuck in the middle, they all fell down and practically kissed (by accident).

When the song ended with Nora waving a limp wand that looked more like a sock than a stick, Isabelle stood up and cheered with everyone else. This was fortitude. This was bravery.

The audience loved it. For a serious person, Nora was really, really funny!

Intermission was almost over when Janet found Isabelle. "There you are," she said. "Samantha needs you. In the girls' room. Now!"

Isabelle ran back to the long row of stalls. Samantha stood there, hands on hips. "This is not what I meant by make her mess up big-time. Do you know that Dee actually told her that she was a genius? That she should ham it up even more in the next act—especially in our big number, which is supposed to feature *me*?"

Isabelle felt bad for Samantha. "I told you to wish to be the best."

"Can't you do something?" Samantha pouted. She paced around the room.

Isabelle felt her wand. She had maybe three or four sparkles left. And maybe Nora's sparkle/glitter (or whatever that was) would run out of juice. She wasn't sure if this was what Grandmomma meant by "the importance of independence" or why Zahara thought "delayed gratification" was so great. Or if these were shenanigans meant to hurt the fairy godmother world.

Isabelle had a strange feeling about Auntie Viv. She was too eccentric to be real.

But right now, Isabelle had to help Samantha. She had to make her happily ever after.

"A wise fairy godmother once told me: You get the right

princess at the right time," Isabelle told Samantha. "And now I understand why." She took a deep breath. What she was about to say was going to be difficult. "So, no. I can't undo what I did. I can't make this easier for you. Samantha, you made your official wish, and that means you have to trust the sparkles. You have everything you need to be happily ever after. And the truth is: I know you can do it, even though Nora is going to keep messing up. So go out there and break a leg! But not really! If you want to be happy, you can do it. You know what that means. And you don't need magic."

In the second act, nothing went according to plan. But it was perfect. Samantha showed as much bravery and fortitude and good humor as Nora.

When Nora tripped, she helped her up.

When Nora forgot a line, Samantha spun in circles and made up great lines a good witch would definitely say.

She even told one of the kids that she couldn't grant his bad wish, because he hadn't yet thought out all the consequences. But in this case, she gave the kid a second chance.

When the play ended, Nora got a standing ovation. Samantha did, too. Together they stood at the center of the stage and bowed.

And then the real magic happened.

They stood together, arms linked. And they both started laughing. When the audience cheered even louder, they gave each other a big hug.

This was the power of sparkles. It was the power of friendship. It was the power of happily ever after.

Isabelle had done it!

When the lights came on, she looked for Auntie Viv. (She really wanted to ask her about those sparkles.) But Isabelle couldn't find her. Not in the audience. Or backstage. Or in the girls' bathroom.

But she did find Samantha. "Are you happy now?" Isabelle asked.

Samantha's stage makeup was smeared and her hair

was almost as messy as Nora's, but it was obvious. She was definitely happy.

"Thanks, Isabelle. I am happily ever after. Nora and I made up. Do you want to go to her house for some post-play cookies?" She told Isabelle she shouldn't say no. "Nora's stepmom is one of the best bakers ever. Even without a fairy godmother. Although, who knows? Maybe she does have one."

This was Isabelle's chance.

All the way to Nora's house (in the car), Isabelle thought about the upcoming Extravaganza. And Angelica and Fawn. Even though she knew returning the sparkles meant admitting her guilt, she was ready to start fresh. She wanted more than anything to be a good fairy godmother. But being a fantastic and loyal granddaughter was even more important. She didn't need a book to teach her that.

It was strange being back at Nora's house.

It was hard pretending that she had never been there before.

But she did it.

And when everyone started singing the big song from the show, Isabelle grabbed a cookie (she couldn't resist) and snuck back to Nora's room.

Isabelle dropped to her knees and wiggled under Nora's bed. Even though the room was well lit, it was dark under there, and it was hard to see. Nora stored her memory box all the way in the back corner. There was also an old birthday card with a smiling elephant on the front, a picture of Samantha and Nora, and a notebook filled with ideas about how to change the world.

Isabelle pulled out the box and sat in the middle of the floor. She had done it. She had made Samantha happily ever after. Nora had her friend back. Everything was going to be great.

Then she opened the box.

The sparkles were gone.

Chapter Nineteen

The Mystery of the Missing Sparkles

No!" Isabelle shouted. "No, no, no, no, no!"

They couldn't be all gone. This couldn't be her fault. It couldn't be that her sparkles had been used to wreck wishes.

But that's what it looked like.

Then she felt a cold and familiar hand on her shoulder. She looked up. She knew that hand.

It was Grandmomma. Dressed like a regular person, with a long coat and a scarf and a snazzy fedora. She did not look happy. Or in the mood for excuses.

Isabelle immediately confessed. "I'm sorry I gave Nora the sparkles. I'm sorry they fell into the wrong hands. I'm sorry that so many things went wrong because of me." Then she confessed all of her secrets, from stealing the sparkles from Grandmomma's office to breaking Rule Three C to giving a couple of sparkles to Nora.

She didn't have to look humble.

She was humble.

All she cared about was the fairy godmother world. "Can you fix this? Can we get the sparkles back? Was Aunt Viv an ex–fairy godmother? What's going to happen to me? Is Mom really in trouble?"

Grandmomma looked at Isabelle in the way that made strong fairy godmothers weak in the knees. "First let's get out of here," she said. "Then we can talk."

Isabelle didn't want to argue. But she did want to say good-bye, even though she knew Samantha and Nora wouldn't remember her tomorrow. This was probably the last wish she'd ever get to grant.

Isabelle looked back through the door. She could see Nora and Samantha singing. And laughing. And flapping Samantha's wings. "Can I just . . ."

"No," Grandmomma said. "If you want to be a fairy godmother, we have to go now."

Isabelle took her grandmomma's arm. She hoped that whatever was going to happen next wouldn't be all that bad. The truth was she was scared, but she was also relieved.

There's nothing worse than keeping a secret for a long time, but some fairy godmothers need to learn things a couple of times.

Even though the Extravaganza was almost ready to start (and fairy godmothers always arrive on time), Grandmomma didn't seem in any rush. First, she took some time to sort through her mail and wiggle her toes. She also couldn't resist a little "I told you so." She *was* a mother, first and foremost.

Then she was ready to lecture Isabelle. "So you understand why we make these rules? And that leaving sparkles unattended will always have very bad consequences?"

Isabelle agreed to everything Grandmomma said. "I have a lot to learn," Isabelle admitted. "But now I know that much."

Grandmomma told Isabelle to stand up. She had something to tell her. She reached into her drawer. Isabelle was sure it was a certificate of banishment. Or a one-way ticket to the Home.

Instead, it was a jar of sparkles. With Isabelle's note still on it.

Isabelle didn't know whether this was nice or mean or positively wonderful. "When did you find them?" Also: "You tricked me!" and "No wonder Nora never wished for me to come back."

Grandmomma looked pleased with Isabelle's response. "Isabelle, who do you think you're dealing with? I got them the night you gave them to Nora." She added, "Why do you think I wasn't in the picture with Clotilda, Angelica, and Fawn?" Grandmomma got up and tried to neaten Isabelle's messy hair. "Did you actually think a fairy god-mother in training could fool the most powerful fairy godmother, who happens to live in the same castle?" When she put it like that, it really did seem ridiculous. "It's a good thing we're family. And that I care so much about the job. And you. Please promise me you won't do that again. It's hard enough dealing with all the real issues in the fairy godmother world without having to defend you to my friends."

"I promise," Isabelle said. Then she asked, "But then whose sparkles were loose? And why didn't you tell me right away?"

Grandmomma didn't answer the first question. She let Clotilda (who was snooping) answer the other. "Because, obviously," Clotilda said, "you're a trainee! We wanted you to learn the hard way. Plus, it was sort of funny watching you try to keep your secret."

That was a little mean, but Isabelle knew she deserved it. "I'm sorry," she said. "But there's one thing I don't understand. Nora had sparkles in her hair. But they weren't magic? Or were they?"

"As far as I know, Nora's magic came completely from her heart," Grandmomma said. "And Aunt Viv's just a nice lady with bad fashion sense and a flair for glitter."

Isabelle wasn't quite sure she believed that. "But she seemed so magical. And lovely. And funny. And those sparkles were so, well, *sparkly*."

"Perhaps she was once a princess?" Clotilda asked.

That was an interesting idea, but Isabelle didn't have time to think about that now. She was too happy. She wasn't in trouble. Plus they had an Extravaganza to attend. "I can still go, can't I?"

"Of course you can," Grandmomma said. "You passed Level Two." Then she added, "Next time something doesn't make sense, trust the sparkles. Use your common sense—not just your gusto. You two are my family. And if there's one thing I've learned over the years, family always comes first."

Grandmomma told them to gather around so she could talk about something really important. In other words, Mom. "When sparkles started disappearing, I hoped that maybe I could find her. But I couldn't."

Isabelle felt sad. "So it was her?"

"I can't say for sure." Grandmomma sighed. Then she sat down. "I had hoped she needed me. I miss her so much."

"I do, too," Clotilda said.

Isabelle said, "And I do, too. Even though I don't remember her at all."

"Isabelle," Grandmomma said, "I know when you gave those sparkles to Nora your intentions were good. But as we have all seen, sparkles can make mischief." She waved her wand and Isabelle's rule book appeared. "So I have a deal for you. I won't tell Luciana about those sparkles. And in return, every day until Level Three, we are going to study together. Do you understand?"

Isabelle understood her vacation was ruined. But she didn't care. This time, she was determined to learn.

"And what about Zahara?" Isabelle asked. "Are you friends again?"

"It might take some time, but I think we'll get there." Grandmomma opened the door. "The last time Zahara hosted an Extravaganza, she gave everyone chocolate shoes. They were delicious! We definitely don't want to miss those."

Chapter Twenty

A Not Quite as Extravagant Extravaganza

*U*nfortunately, Zahara did not have enough sparkles to make chocolate shoes.

But she did have enough to turn the ballroom into a lush and beautiful enchanted garden, complete with trails covered in moss, as well as all kinds of flowers and shrubs. Isabelle admired how the walls looked like sunshine. The girlgoyles looked gorgeous in their flower wreaths.

"It looks beautiful," she told Zahara. The old woman was dressed in a long flowing dress covered with real flowers. She picked two flowers right off her dress and handed them to the sisters. "Go on, eat them. They're actually pretty tasty!"

Before Grandmomma could say anything, she added, "And welcome home, my friend." At first they just stood there. Then they shook hands. Then Isabelle shouted, "Hug already!" So they did. And then everyone laughed, because Grandmomma was tall and Zahara was tiny and they looked funny hugging and laughing in their fancy clothes.

Since they had a lot of catching up to do (which might have included an invitation to teach again in training), Isabelle decided it was a good time to explore. She walked down the path and admired all the exotic flowers. Then she found an actual wishing well (still not magic), made a wish, and poured herself a cup of sparkling raspberry juice. To her surprise, right in front of her was a gigantic gnarly tree just like the one she had planted. It was even covered with pink blossoms! And right behind it was the buffet.

The food looked wonderful and natural (if maybe a tad on the healthy side). There were cucumber sandwiches with the crusts cut off, flower-shaped cookies, muffins stuffed with blueberries, and tiny scones and cakes that tasted like they were filled with mango cream. Just as Isabelle was about to eat her first chocolate-covered strawberry, Luciana came over to congratulate her. "I knew you could make those regular girls happily ever after. Now I hope you will eat and dance and celebrate that we fairy godmothers can do anything! Having fortitude isn't about being unhappy. It's about trusting yourself. And, of course, the sparkles. When you want to make a princess or regular girl happy, you have to believe in their power. Am I right or what!" She patted Isabelle on the head and handed her another edible flower. "I have an idea. Why don't you give this to Angelica?"

Isabelle understood what she was saying. To Isabelle's surprise, she found Angelica at the other end of the buffet, filling her plate with enough sandwiches for three trainees.

They traded treats. "I heard you got a standing ovation," Angelica said.

She was still wearing her necklace. And it was still bright red. When Isabelle stepped back, Angelica said, "It's never not red," and she looked sincerely humble. "Either my magic is on the fritz, or everyone has secrets. I just think it's pretty." (This was her way of unofficially burying the hatchet.)

When Fawn came over to say hello, they all shook hands. And then they all raised their wands and touched them together. They shouted, "H.E.A. forever!" Then Isabelle asked both girls for an update. (This was her way of burying the hatchet and accepting their apologies.)

Angelica said, "Even though my first practice princess lost her big race and her boat, she was a good sport. She immediately started saving for a new boat, and then she challenged my second practice princess to a rematch."

She thought about it for a minute. "I think they're going to be friends, too."

Fawn thought Isabelle and Angelica got off easy. "My snowstorm was terrible. But I guess, like your wishes, it brought a lot of people together."

Together, they tried the edible flower lollipops, five kinds of cheese, and a slice of tropical-fruit pizza. Even when fairy godmothers conserve sparkles, they are very good in the kitchen. Isabelle made a big plate of food and went to look for the Worsts.

They were at their back table, complaining as usual.

For them, the food was too fresh. The theme was too obvious. The whole fortitude and focus experiment still made them mad. Plus they were always cold. The draft from the back door still hadn't been repaired. They didn't even say thank you for the plate.

But none of that mattered because Minerva was there. "I'm so glad to see you," Isabelle said.

"So you heard I didn't grant her wish," Minerva said.

Isabelle nodded. "Do you know what's going to happen next?"

She said, "Not a clue, and I don't care. They'll probably put me on what they call 'secret' probation." She put air quotes around *secret* since probation wasn't secret at all.

This was a lot of gusto for one old godmother—especially a Worst. "What did they ask you to do?"

Minerva told her, "They wanted me to grant the wish of the missing relative of my first practice princess—to bring them all together. But since I have known the family a long time, I knew this would mean trouble. If I had intervened, everyone would have found out that my first long-ago princess wasn't born a princess at all. And that neither were her descendants."

"Wait a minute," Isabelle said. "I thought I got the first regular girl."

Minerva shook her head. "Isabelle, the history of fairy godmothering is a long one. It is also filled with new rules, broken rules, and sometimes, forgotten secrets. There are plenty of princesses who started out as regular girls. They just don't like to talk about it in training."

Isabelle figured she'd better get reading. But right now, she was more worried about what was going to happen to Minerva.

"Isabelle, a lot of us have been thinking. We love being godmothers, but the system works against us. We really aren't *Worsts*." She pointed to Grandmomma and the Bests. "Do you really think we're ever going to get a shot at a really good princess?"

At the podium, Grandmomma held up her hand so that everyone would stop talking. "Welcome, friends! I am so glad to see all of you." As always, she introduced the Bests, numbers one through four.

Then all the godmothers who needed princesses joined Grandmomma onstage. It was very exciting when Clotilda (who could have chosen anyone) passed on a very easy-to-please princess and instead chose a difficult princess who had already stumped four fairy godmothers.

"I'm up for the challenge," Clotilda told the room full of cheering godmothers.

Minerva whispered to Isabelle, "And so am I!" She stood up slowly—not to clap, but to do the limbo. She arched her back until it crackled and popped. "Just in case this is my last Extravaganza, let's make it a doozy!"

Isabelle went to find Clotilda. First she congratulated Clotilda on her excellent taste in difficult princesses.

Then they did the limbo. Then Grandmomma stopped the music. It was time for a class picture. (She didn't want Isabelle to miss this one.) Isabelle stood in front of the tree with Zahara, the Bests, and her classmates for an official Level Two graduation picture.

"Congratulations," Grandmomma said.

"Sparkle power!" they shouted together.

Chapter Twenty-One

Sisters!

After three servings of food, four conga lines, three electric slides, and sixteen (or so) rounds of the chicken dance, Isabelle was ready to go home. She asked Clotilda, "You want to come up and say hi to the girlgoyles?"

It had been a long time since Clotilda had joined her with the girlgoyles—maybe since before Clotilda started training. "Sure," she said. "Let's do it."

It took them a little while to get comfortable, but eventually, they squeezed in tight. For a while, they counted constellations. Then they watched a star shoot across the sky. Behind one of the girlgoyles, Isabelle discovered a half-eaten bag of pretzels. They ate them all up even though they were really stale.

If there was one thing stronger than the magic of sparkles, it was the magic of sisterhood. It even made stale pretzels taste delicious.

"So tell me the truth. Did you think it was Mom?" Isabelle asked.

Clotilda shook her head. "Never. No way. Mom wasn't like that. People can say whatever they like, but I knew her. She would never do anything to hurt a princess—or a regular girl."

That made Isabelle feel a little better, but now that she had her sister cornered and squished, she also had a lot of other questions. Like: "Why couldn't she take us with her?" and "Do you think Grandmomma really didn't find her?" and "Why didn't she leave us anything to remember her by?"

Clotilda didn't know where their mom was. And she liked being a fairy godmother. She told Isabelle she wouldn't have wanted to leave, either. Then Clotilda pointed out the same special star that Isabelle always looked at when she wanted to think about Mom. "You were too young to remember, but before she left, she told us that when we missed her, we should throw a sparkle in the air. Like a shooting star. And that she would see it. She said that shooting stars always made wishes more powerful."

"*She* taught us that?" (Isabelle thought she'd made that up herself.)

Clotilda laughed. "You think Grandmomma would teach us to waste sparkles? That is not her style."

That was true. And sort of funny. And at the same time, really sad. "You want to do it right now?" Isabelle asked. (She had exactly two extra sparkles left in her wand.)

So they each took one. And they launched them high into the sky. And even though they didn't say anything more, they both thought about Mom. They didn't have to say they'd always stick together. But Isabelle knew they would.

After a while, Clotilda stood up. (The cozy space was really too cozy for two fairy godmothers. It was really only right for one.) She said, "Don't stay too long" and "Like I always say: Be calm. Grandmomma has a big day in store for you tomorrow."

Isabelle said good night. "I'll be just a minute." She wanted to be alone, especially because now she didn't feel lonely.

Also, she thought she saw something sparkly on the claw of one of the girlgoyles. When Clotilda was gone, Isabelle reached for it. It was a little yellow-and-green ring.

Isabelle was pretty sure Clotilda had left it for her. For good luck. A keepsake. Maybe it had even been Mom's.

Isabelle put it on her finger and looked up at the big, bright star. It seemed to be twinkling now, like it was saying: "I am out here. Don't forget me." And of course, "Make a wish." Since what else can you do with a twinkling star, even if you are an almost Level Three fairy godmother and you don't have a fairy godmother of your own?

So Isabelle held her hand and her ring to her heart. And she made a wish. Of course, this was Isabelle we're talking about, so it was a complicated wish. That was because she wanted too many things. And because she was still too disorganized. She would have to talk to Grandmomma about that tomorrow.

She wished that:

a) Nora and Samantha would stay happy. And that they would continue to be friends. And that maybe, somehow, she could see them again. But if not, she was all right with that.

b) If there were regular girls who were princesses in disguise, that it should be one of them. She also wouldn't mind getting another regular girl in Level Three.

c) Minerva would come back to training. And not be on probation.

Of course, Isabelle also wanted to see her mom and make it through Level Three and finally be really good friends with Angelica and Fawn (in other words: the kind who worked together and needed each other), but that was getting ridiculous and mushy, so she just added d) all of the above and everything else.

What she didn't know (but probably should have):

Rings don't appear out of nowhere, even in the fairy godmother world. When rings (or other jewels) show up, it means that there is strong magic happening. Or as fairy godmothers like to say, something is afoot.

It's as dangerous as giving sparkles to a regular girl. Anything can happen.

Acknowledgments

If there is one thing stronger than the magic of sparkles, it's the magic of story and what happens when you forget your fears and try something totally new and exciting. I hope this book is as fun to read as it was to write!

I cannot say thank you enough. Honestly, there are days when I'm sure it's not real! What a joy these books are for me!

First and foremost to my amazing team at Scholastic, especially Anna Bloom, AnnMarie Anderson, Abby McAden, Maeve Norton, and extra special kudos to the copyeditor, Jessica White. I'm pretty sure I owe you dinner out. All of your feedback and patience and enthusiasm helped me find this next chapter in Isabelle's story and get it right. As always, I owe my agent, Sarah Davies, so much for all her support, trust, wisdom, and well-timed humor. VCFA, the Highlights Foundation, SCBWI, and writers.com: Thank you for all the opportunities and communities you have provided.

I wouldn't be writing this without the continued support of friends from my writing world and the regular one, too. (You know who you are!!!) Every day, I feel lucky that we're in this together!

Huge thanks to my writing sisters, Tami Lewis Brown, Elly Swartz, and Tanya Lee Stone, as well as my daughter/on-call idea consultant, Rebecca Aronson, who helped me sift through good paragraphs, clunkers, as well as everything else life offers. My critique group has been a great source of inspiration and creative chutzpah! Thank you, Carolyn Crimi, Jenny Meyerhoff, Mary Loftus, Brenda Ferber, and Laura Ruby, for giving me the weekly doses of confidence I've needed.

Thank you to my family, especially my husband, Michael, and son, Elliot, who tell me every single day that I can do this.

It has been wonderful to be given the chance to write and share stories about fairy godmothers and happiness. I am so grateful to have this opportunity. Most days, I have to pinch myself!

Sparkle on!

About the Author

Sarah Aronson has always believed in magic—especially when it comes to writing. Her favorite things (in no particular order) include all kinds of snacks (especially chocolate), sparkly accessories, biking along Lake Michigan, and reading all kinds of stories—just not the fine print!

Sarah holds an MFA in Writing for Children and Young Adults from Vermont College of Fine Arts. She lives with her family in Evanston, Illinois.

Find out more at www.saraharonson.com.

Author photo by Lynn Bohannon